A WILD RIDE

Shellene Ramsahoye

Copyright © 2018 by Shellene Ramsahoye.

ISBN   Softcover   978-1-948801-92-8

All rights reserved. No part of this book may be reproduced or transmitted in any form or by any means, electronic or mechanical, including photocopying, recording, or by any information storage and retrieval system without express written permission from the author, except in the case of brief quotations embodied in critical reviews and certain other non-commercial uses permitted by copyright law.

Printed in the United States of America.

Bookwhip
106 Commodore Terrace
Edgewater, NJ 07020

CHAPTER 1

Fourteen-year-old Justin absently twisted the frayed strings on his grey hoodie while staring out the Jeep window. Endless pine trees whizzed past as he and his father made their way up the winding mountain road. The dense underbrush barely admitted daylight and altogether the forest stood firm like a sentinel guarding the mountain's secrets.

The only things that penetrated the unbreaking perimeter of trees were the occasional deep, jagged ravines and slopes that threatened of falling rocks.

Sure wouldn't want to be lost in all that bush, thought Justin. He squashed his already tousled brown hair against the headrest, rotating his neck until he was somewhat comfortable. He stretched as far out as possible, jamming his hiking boots to the very front end of the Grand Cherokee's floor mats. Sleep was impossible, though, as there was no way of predicting when the next pothole would jostle him awake.

But Dad jumped in before the next pothole could.

"Camp will be great," Dad said without taking his eyes off the road. "Just think how prepared you'll be for the annual Attwood family hunting trip in November." Every year with great ceremony, three generations of the Attwood clan would trek into a northerly wooded location and harvest several of the best deer they could possibly find. "We'll hang your first deer mount right next to Jason's in the front foyer."

Naturally his older brother Jason's buck was immense, something about a record score of antler points. Jason always excelled, no matter what he did. He'd make a really driven lawyer in the next few years. Even Justin's sister, Sabrina, had shot a pretty doe one year, just to prove men weren't the only part of the human species that had the skill to hunt. But since Sabrina didn't prefer venison no matter how it was cooked, she promptly arranged to donate her deer to 'hunters for the hungry'. The next year she very effectively excused herself by saying now that she had tried it once, she knew she shouldn't be killing something she didn't eat.

Justin wondered if shooting a squirrel and donating it to his biology lab would be a suitable enough first attempt in Dad's record book to excuse him.

Dad kept trying. "You might even surprise Granddad and me and get a bigger one than Jason's."

"Maybe." Apparently Dad was satisfied with that answer and didn't seem to catch Justin's lack of enthusiasm for the hunting trip. Justin wasn't even certain he wanted to kill a deer. He'd always admired photographs of them – deer were so athletic and capable in their environment. Who was Justin to decide if that particular deer should be killed? Wasn't that Mother Nature's job – survival of the fittest and all?

Justin's thoughts of being fit and fitting in wandered to what his friends were doing back at home. They were probably down at the skateboard park, or maybe a quick game of three-on-three at the sport complex. Justin's wrist motioned a quick flick as he envisioned the perfect three-point release. Now these were the kind of sports he could understand.

His visualization of a breathtaking breakaway move was broken by a glimpse of the sign – "Wapiti Junction Wilderness Camp – 5km". Five more kilometers of uneven terrain and the possibility of Dad talking more about hunting, Justin thought. The camp was barely part way up the mountain but the altitude change was high enough to feel chilly, even in early August. A shiver crawled up Justin's back and he stuffed his fists into his hoodie's pockets.

The gravel crackled under the Jeep's tires as they pulled into the camp parking lot. Parking spots were peppered with various 4X4's and SUV's outfitted with heavy-duty bumpers, winches and racks, likely a testimony to the unpredictable nature of the weather up here. The vehicles almost seemed tethered to the thick round logs outlining the lot like horses in an old Western. Surrounding the lot were carefully constructed cabins nestled in a mixed green treeline as the jagged blue-white mountain range rose in the background. The camp's brochure noted that these cabins doubled as a cross-country skiing and snowshoe retreat in the winter months.

In any season this place was right off a postcard or a National Geographic cover, Justin thought. He unfolded his lanky frame out the passenger door and stretched his inactive muscles. He rounded the Jeep to help Dad heft out his gear.

"That's a lot of kit." Justin leaned past the lift door to see a sandy-haired boy about his age casually surveying the pile of duffel bags.

"I'm Shawn Miller." He readily stepped forward to help, taking Justin's backpack from the Jeep and heaping it on the pile. "I bet you're my roommate. Mike said there was one more guy to come, so you must be him."

"I guess so. I'm Justin Attwood, and this is my dad." Justin wished he felt as relaxed as this guy looked.

"If I'd known you were bringing all this stuff, I'd have spent less time packing," Shawn said, grinning. Shawn looked like he already belonged in this place with his khaki cargo shorts and loosely-laced hiking boots. Or maybe he'd fit better down at the beach with a surfboard. Either way, Justin found himself feeling less apprehensive about camp.

"Hey, Shawn! Looks like you've already met your cabin mate." An athletic man in his mid-twenties waved his clipboard and jogged down from the main cabin. "Justin, it's great to have you here." He then offered his hand to Justin's dad. "Mr. Attwood. I'm Mike Chamberlain. I'll be the boys' main instructor for the next two weeks."

Justin stood by Shawn, quietly checking out his surroundings, while Mike and Dad chatted briefly. From what he could tell, they were parked right in front of the main building because it carried all the major signs and site maps. Behind it a graveled trail branched off to a split-section building that announced its purpose with a huge antlered creature the color of snow-free mountains carved into its cedar sign – 'Blue Moose Food'. Now he was pretty sure he knew where the dining hall was.

Beyond that, more trails dispersed to cabins that were harder to see because of the thick, towering pine trees. Dad's voice jolted his attention back to the parking lot.

"Well, Justin, you seem to be in good hands. I'll take off now," Dad said. He gave Justin a quick embrace and clap on the back. "See you in two weeks!" Justin had barely blinked once when all he could see were the Jeep's taillights heading down the trail.

"Come on, Justin, we'll get you settled in. It's almost time for the orientation session," Mike said, easily shouldering two bags from the pile, as the boys grabbed the rest.

They walked into the impressive main building. It appeared even larger on the inside due to an open beam ceiling and intricate, interlacing log half-walls defining each corner. Several other instructors milled around an office while other campers lounged on squishy leather couches around a fire, which flickered and crackled in a stone pit in the center of the room.

They dropped Justin's gear just inside the entrance way. "We meet here in the main building everyday to organize each activity or training session," Mike explained to the boys. Have a seat and we'll get started with the orientation."

There were five instructors besides Mike, three more men and two women. The activities they described during the orientation sounded exactly like the brochure. The thirty-two campers present would be split into teams and rotate through all the training stations – rock climbing, rappelling, hiking, rafting/canoeing, wilderness first aide, survival skills, local plants and animals and orienteering.

"But don't get too comfortable in here," said Carrie, one of the women instructors who spoke the most about the local plants and animals. "To start things off we're headed on a hike around the entire camp grounds so you get familiar with where you'll be training." She smiled as many whoops were heard around the room.

Maybe I will get to see what's behind all those trees. A wall of trees protected the road to camp and an enclosure of pines surrounding the cabins. *What were they shielding anyway?*

"We'll only be hiking the main marked trails," Carrie continued like she could hear inside Justin's head. "People unfamiliar with these woods have been lost for days after venturing off the main trails."

The excited stirring of the campers immediately raised the noise level in the main hall. Carrie raised her arm to get one last bit of attention. "Get your gear – better hope those hiking boots are well broken in, or you'll have blisters tonight! Don't forget to pack your water bottles and binoculars in your light packs. Meet you back here in 15 minutes."

Shawn helped Justin grab his gear. "Guess we won't be wasting any time sitting around here thinking," Shawn said, grinning his infectious grin.

"That's probably a good thing," Justin answered, shaking off his last moments with Dad and jogging after Shawn toward their cabin.

CHAPTER 2

It took exactly 24 hours for Justin to feel like he'd been friends with Shawn all his life and to wish that Todd Baker and Steven Ashbrook would fall down a cliff.

Todd and Steven were the kind of guys that Justin steered clear of at school and sports – everything faster, higher, farther – spare no cost. And typically, they got away with pushing the edge and were even congratulated for it.

He suspected Dad would have appreciated him more if he were more like these guys. Too bad Justin felt he was on the opposite end of the spectrum.

He preferred Shawn's more relaxed approach. Not that he didn't put in his best effort, but he planned and was cautious but not to the point of fearful. It was more like Shawn was a natural athlete whose skills came easily to him and he knew how far he could go. Now, Justin could get behind that attitude.

And behind it, he was.

"Justin, you're swinging the ropes!" Shawn called shakily over his shoulder. Shawn was first in line on the suspension bridge awaiting an instructor to supervise the activity.

Well, maybe a little fear was a motivating thing. "Sorry, I'll hold back for a bit until you get going," Justin answered, amused at Shawn's surprising hesitation at the suspension rope exercise. The swinging rope bridge was as safe as any of the camp activities – harnesses, guide lines, safety ropes – it just wasn't exactly still.

His amusement was short-lived. "What's the matter, Miller, scared of heights?" Todd taunted from the bottom of the ladder.

Justin instantly felt his blood boil. He took a deep breath in hopes of controlling his urge to jump down and punch the loudmouth.

"Ignore them," Justin said to Shawn in a low voice. "Don't give them the satisfaction of an answer."

Justin dropped back more so his body weight didn't sway the ropes against Shawn's rhythm. Shawn set his shoulders, determined to make it across with at least a small bit of finesse.

"Hey, Attwood, maybe you should hold his hand!" Steven yelled.

Justin shot a withering glance behind him but managed to hold his tongue. *What was with these guys? What did we do to them in just one day?*

Todd and Steven clammed up immediately. Their wilderness instructor, Mike, finished talking with another instructor and walked over to the waiting campers. "Hope you boys are ready down here," he said. Mike casually eyed Todd and Steven but said nothing else. He turned his attention to Shawn at the front of the line.

"Just let yourself go with the sway of the ropes. It'll go easier if you don't fight it," he called up to Shawn. Mike split his attention between Shawn's progress and Todd and Steven's apparent discomfort.

Justin felt more relaxed with Mike's arrival. His focus shifted to his own turn at the ropes. Shawn had successfully adjusted his body motion to work with the ropes rather than against them and made it across without needing to rely on the safety measures. Justin followed his friend to the end of the exercise.

"Good work, boys," Mike said, giving them both a pat on the back. "Get back in line, and we'll try it again." He smiled as Shawn hung his head and laughed.

Justin glanced up as Todd and Steven were preparing to cross. He noticed their attempts to ignore attaching the safety ropes to their harnesses. He wondered if Mike would see it from the ground.

"OK, next in line! Make sure your safety gear is engaged – fifteen feet is a long way to the ground," Mike yelled up to Todd and Steven. "If you can't hook it yourself, I can climb up to give you a hand."

Justin smiled inwardly. *Guess that's my answer. Maybe there is some justice in the world.*

But the good-natured competition that continued through the rest of the suspension bridge exercise did not carry over to the dining hall. Todd and Steven sat back-to-back with Justin and Shawn at the long parallel picnic benches and picked up where they left off before Mike arrived.

Todd leaned back between Justin and Shawn. "Must be nice to be so tight with Mike." He stuffed a french fry into his mouth. "He almost needed to talk you down from the bridge."

"Lay off, Todd," Shawn answered, swallowing his bite of hamburger. "Use your mouth to chew your food."

Todd swirled another fry in his ketchup and looked thoughtful. "It's probably good for Attwood to have a father-figure like Mike around. Considering his own dad sped out of here once he was finally free of him." He grinned smugly at the cleverness of his comment.

Justin was so stunned, his burger-filled hand stopped halfway to his mouth. *I thought no one but Mike and Shawn were around when Dad dropped me off. Just my luck this idiot was around to see it.* He squared off to look Todd right in the eye.

"You spend a lot of time worrying about the stuff we do. Don't you have anything interesting in your own life to keep you busy?" Justin was amazed at himself. He couldn't believe these calm, collected words rolled out despite having the same blood-boiling feeling that washed over him earlier.

"Burgers make great take-out food," Shawn said, gathering his dinner and sliding out of the bench. Justin grabbed his food and quickly followed Shawn while it was Todd's turn to be stunned into silence.

Back at their cabin, Justin and Shawn loaded their backpacks for the next day between bites of burgers and fries. Tomorrow's exercise included hiking up the same 'hill' they explored the first day complete with trail maps and a mini climb at the top. Holding his burger in one hand, Justin dug around in his duffel bag with his free hand for a pair of thicker socks to fit snugly into his hiking boots. He fished out a pair he liked and sat down on the floor to finish his burger.

"What is with those guys?" Justin asked.

Shawn tossed his empty water bottle on his cot and slid his plate of food down to the floor. "I remember now where I've seen Todd before. He was at scouting camp with me a few years back." Shawn munched a fry thoughtfully. "Even then he was one of those guys who could do most everything but made sure people knew how good he was."

"It's getting harder for me to ignore him," Justin said. He slipped his own water bottle into the netted side pocket of his pack. "I wish Todd and Steven would get shifted to another group."

"That's not going to happen because I think we've all been matched based on our skills. So we'll just keep out of their way and just be faster and cleaner than them."

Justin raised his eyebrows and snorted. "Sure, that will be no problem."

The boys finished cleaning up and crawled into their bunks. Justin could hear Shawn breathing deeply within a few minutes, but he was not so lucky.

He stared at the knotty pine ceiling, rolling over multiple fantastical scenarios about how he heroically could rid himself of evil Todd and his minion, Steven. None, however, were likely to happen, especially the one dealing with spontaneous combustion during an overheated hike.

Shawn was right. *The only way to get the best of these guys was to learn the skills properly, do them quickly and have a good time while doing it. Just that simple. Now if I could convince myself of that the next time Todd ticks me off.*

With this plan loosely in place, Justin drifted into an uneasy sleep filled with fragmented dreams. About midnight he startled himself awake. In his dream Dad mounted Todd's trophy buck on the Attwood family hunting wall of fame.

After a quick and uneventful breakfast the campers assembled to hike the mapped areas on the hill they hiked with Carrie on the first day. Carrie called the group together to explain the exercise.

"The hill has been split into several trails with varying degrees of difficulty and length," Carrie began. "Each two-person team will be given a map so they could choose a suitable trail depending on their skill and endurance in advance. The trails are marked at regular intervals with surveyor's tape for safety, should anyone need help."

The climbing instructor, Andrew, stepped forward to describe the rest of the exercise. "The summit of the hike ends in a mini rock climb," Andrew said, pointing up the hill. "Each team will harness themselves into their safety equipment, climb the gradual surface for about 10 feet to a taped line and then rappel down. After unharnessing, the only thing left is to hike down any of the marked trails." Andrew stopped to see if there were any questions. With all eyes on him, he continued. "At all times you will to stick close to your partner and use teamwork to complete the circuit as cleanly and safely as possible." Andrew emphasized this instruction by looking at each camper directly.

Justin saw Todd and Steven shift slightly but quickly averted his eyes so not to draw their attention. He focused on Andrew again.

"Instructors will be stationed along the circuit using check sheets to see what skills each team demonstrates effectively and what needs some work," Andrew continued. "For those interested, the circuit will be timed, but only for personal comparisons."

Again it was Carrie's turn for a few final words. "Make sure your packs have what you need – water, snack, extra socks, laces, climbing gloves – all the necessities," she said. "Keep your maps somewhere on your body and stick to the marked trails. We don't need to call in the search and rescue technicians on your third day here!"

Through everyone's giggles, Justin heard Steven cough. *No doubt he was choking down a hard laugh at one of Todd's asinine comments. Probably at either my or Shawn's expense*, he thought grimly. Justin's restless sleep filled with images of Todd did nothing for his plan about ignoring him during his waking hours. His tolerance nerves were already raw.

Justin was able to refocus after spending some time in map review and thinking of a good strategy with Shawn. Each team then began the trek in staggered starts up the trails. Justin and Shawn chose a moderately challenging trail that was quite straight to the top of the circuit but with uneven terrain. They set out at a good pace and frequently referenced their hand-held compass in relation to the map and trail markers.

The less foot-friendly trail they had chosen was peppered with loose rocks of variable shapes and sizes that caused them several stumbles and ankle twists. The morning dew still held on to the smoother rocks out of direct sunlight leaving a slippery surface for even the best of hiking boots. The tangling low brush crowding the spruce tree trunks scraped at their legs and grabbed at their bootlaces.

Not much farther along the way they had met Mike with his clipboard, who waved them on with a nod and a thumbs-up. With this feedback and being experienced hikers, Justin and Shawn picked their way carefully, arriving at the climb in good time.

Andrew was waiting at the climb. "Welcome, boys. You're my first guinea pigs of the day," he said, smiling broadly. "Let's get you into your harnesses, helmets and hook-ups."

The climb was one designed for even the least experienced climber. The distance and slope kept the climber close to the ground, and the rock sizes ranged from medium to large. This type of climb allowed Andrew to judge everyone's skills with handgrips, footwork, balance and movement on the rocks. Justin had done some climbing at the local recreation center but very little outdoors. He was happy the harnessing was similar to that used at the suspensions climb.

He guessed that equipment was modified from what was used in rock climbing. The ease of climb was one that let them wear their hiking boots instead of changing to climbing shoes. He and Shawn harnessed up quickly. They decided Shawn would go first with Justin watching the safeguards.

Justin could tell Shawn had more experience climbing. He confidently chose his holds and was able to move his body effectively up the slope to the tape. He slapped the rough rock face with his hand and looked back at Justin to get ready for his descent.

"Coming down, buddy," he called, adjusting his rope behind him.

"I've got your back," Justin replied.

Shawn used his guide ropes to rappel smoothly and swiftly down the climb surface. Justin watched how Shawn placed his feet to try to improve his own technique. Shawn landed at the base with a gratified smile on his face and a "Good work" from Andrew. Shawn and Justin readied themselves to switch places.

Justin's climb was not as smooth or speedy, but he felt he made good decisions about where to place his feet and hands. Andrew kept a watchful eye and called some words of encouragement as he kept himself well balanced as he slapped the tape mark at the top. Justin was beginning to feel pleased with himself as he signaled to Shawn he was ready to come down. Thinking about Shawn's descent, Justin used his body's motion fluidly with the rock's irregular surface to make it smoothly to the ground.

"Awesome, dude," Shawn said, as the two stripped off their harnesses and strapped on their packs for the trip down. They waved at Andrew who was hooking up another team. They checked their map to decide which trail to take back down.

"If we take the one we came up on, we should get back in great time," Justin said, also thinking that they might even beat Todd and Steven's time.

"It was pretty moist on the way up. It might still be slippery on the way down," Shawn said as he considered some of the other trails' features. "But if we watch our footing we'll probably get down OK." He folded up the map and tucked it in the cargo pocket of his khaki shorts.

Shawn was right. Even though it was later in the morning the sun still had not fully penetrated the dense canopy of the mixed forest to dry out the underbrush. The moss and small plants that clung to the soil and rocks held on tightly to the morning dew. The footing was slick in places. To see better, both boys rested their sunglasses on their ball caps and kept a close watch on the ever-changing ground surface. Justin was concentrating so hard he barely missed stepping on a small red squirrel skittering through the deadfall.

"Ho! Sorry little guy," he said, stopping suddenly to let the squirrel pass. The little rodent chattered angrily at him as it scurried by.

Shawn laughed. "I'm not sure which one of you was the most surprised."

"Yeah, I guess I was in my zone, thinking about not wiping out." He wiped his forehead with the band on his wrist and looked up the path taken by the sure-footed squirrel. Justin collected himself in time to move aside for a team of girls about their age to pass. They gave the boys an odd glance on their way past.

"Watch out for the attack squirrels on this trail," Justin suggested.

"Don't worry, we will," the taller blonde girl assured with a wave.

"Nice," Shawn said, shaking his head. "Now that you're done checking out the wildlife, let's get going."

By this time Justin was feeling more confident than he had for the whole circuit. He and Shawn talked of all the animals and sights they had seen on previous hikes and managed to keep a good pace descending the marked trail. A quick consultation of map and compass showed that they had only two turns before they reached the bottom. Coming around the first turn Shawn stepped off trail to avoid a mossy rock section of trail. As he dodged the slippery ground cover a flurry of feathers rushed up at his face. He raised his arms to protect his face as the hard-beating wings swerved toward Justin.

"Whoa!" Justin sidestepped his second surprise animal for the day and felt his foot slide out from underneath him on the moss-covered rocks. Attempting to recover, he shifted his leg to regain his balance and quick stabbing pain went through his twisted knee. He hissed through his teeth at the sudden pain. Instantly, he sat on the ground clutching his knee.

"Sorry, man, are you all right?" Shawn asked. "I didn't mean to send that grouse in your direction."

"I think my knee is just twisted," Justin answered, massaging his knee. "I guess I'm not having much luck with animals today."

"Do you want me to check your knee?" Shawn offered. "I've done tons of first aid training when I worked as a scouting camp assistant."

"Thanks, but I think I can walk it off. Besides, we're almost finished," Justin said, feeling the discomfort subside a little.

Shawn helped him to his feet and got him started. They walked slowly at first until the leg warmed up. By the time they reached the bottom of the climb, Justin was able to move the knee through all motions without pain.

At the finish point the boys squeezed their water bottles for a good long drink.

Mike approached them with a congratulatory smile. "Good work, guys. You made excellent time and Andrew said your climbing skills were quite good," he said, checking his clipboard. "You ready to go again?"

"Um, sure," Justin answered, glancing at Shawn. Mike caught their look and paused for an explanation.

"I twisted my right knee just before we came around that last bend on the trail. It feels a bit stiff, but I think I can work through it," Justin explained.

Mike had Justin sit for a quick check. He grabbed two ice packs from the cooler and iced both sides of Justin's knee. After a few minutes Mike pulled a tensor bandage from one of the on-site first aid kits and carefully wrapped the knee.

"How does that feel?" Mike asked, examining his 'field dressing'.

"Great. It doesn't feel stiff anymore," Justin said, flexing his knee. "I think I'm ready for another run."

Mike hesitated. "All right, but if it feels sore again, especially during the climb, just stop for today. And check in with the nurse when we're done here."

"Thanks, Mike," Justin said. He and Shawn grabbed their packs and headed up a more forgiving trail Shawn had chosen on the map while Mike tended Justin's knee.

The second trip through the circuit was far less eventful.

Justin took it easier, and managed a decent climb and rappel. They arrived at the bottom of the circuit with a greater total time, but a clean run, considering Justin's injury. They waited at the rendezvous point while the remaining hikers completed their runs.

Andrew whistled loudly through his fingers and each team gathered around the instructors. "Terrific job, everyone! After lunch we'll head down to the lake to swim for the afternoon. We'll bring each team's hiking and climbing checklists to review with you between jumps off the swinging rope."

Justin was grateful for the break. He hated to admit it, but his knee was feeling a bit robotic. He paused outside the dining hall. "I'd better stop in to see the nurse before lunch, like Mike said," he said to Shawn.

"OK, I'll go grab us a spot," Shawn answered, flowing with the other campers toward the smell of food wafting from the kitchen.

Justin's visit to the nurse was routine. He waited on a wood sculpted futon covered in moose-patterned cushions while she finished dressing a rock rash on the arm of another girl in his section. Within a few minutes of re-icing, checking, re-wrapping and instructions on taking some anti-inflammatory tablets, Justin was off to lunch. The nurse had suggested that he rest on the lounge chairs instead of swimming this afternoon, but if he really wanted to go he could come back and have his knee wrapped again. She discharged him after she was satisfied that his rest and recovery would be good. Canoeing was on the schedule for tomorrow, so it would be mostly arm work instead of leg work.

His leg almost felt normal as he stepped up the stairs to the Blue Moose. *Mmm, macaroni and cheese day*, he noted, grabbing a tray and filling his plate. Juggling his pasta plate, milk and cookies, he slid into to the bench spot Shawn had saved for him. Not far away Todd and Steven were keenly observing his late arrival and bandaged leg.

"Can't they ever mind their own business?" Justin whispered to Shawn, who was enthusiastically cleaning his plate with the remnants of a buttered slice of bread.

Shawn shifted seamlessly to his chocolate chip cookies while Justin wolfed down his lunch. "Forget them," he said, still chewing. "Let's get our stuff and get down to the lake."

Sitting during lunch allowed time for some stiffness to settle into Justin's knee. With reluctance, he decided he'd rather go canoeing tomorrow than swimming today, so he made a beeline for a deck chair on the floating pier. Mike was on lifeguard duty and pointed at Justin's bandaged knee with a slight frown. Justin motioned toward the deck chair and received a nod of approval from Mike. He almost changed his mind about swimming as he watched Shawn swing out wide over the lake's glassy surface on the tree rope and cannonball with a huge splash. His knee twinged when he readjusted his legs, so he resigned himself to his Gatorade and new comic book he brought from home.

His reverie was broken when Todd washed up noisily onto the deck next to his chair.

"Can't swim, or do you really have a sore leg?" Todd taunted. "Probably that beginner course was too much for you this morning."

"Shawn and I could beat your team any day, Todd," Justin answered, not looking up from his comic, "even with my twisted knee."

"Doubt it. Hey, that's probably why your Dad dropped you off in such a hurry. The sooner you get practicing the sooner you might get good at something." Todd smiled thinly.

Justin instantly felt the heat rise inside him and hoped it didn't show on his face. He was about to retaliate when Shawn hopped up beside Todd.

"Need a break already, Baker?" Shawn asked smoothly, flipping his soaking blonde hair out of his eyes and spraying Todd in the process.

Justin had enough time to straighten his argument. "We'll beat your times on the circuit, no problem." It was a weak comment, but at least he didn't sound too rattled.

"How about a challenge tonight, then, if you're not too scared?" Todd asked casually, as if he hadn't just suggested they break one of the camp rules.

Shawn slowly screwed the top on his own sports drink. "If we hit the trails without supervision, we could get kicked out of camp, Todd. You know that."

Todd rolled his eyes at Shawn and turned back to Justin. "No wonder Dad's disappointed – you'll never get to the top by playing by the rules." He eyed Justin carefully to see if his comments had found their mark. "Besides, the trails are already marked, and we have maps. We could be in and out before dark with no one noticing – unless you're not as fast as you say."

"Oh, you'll find out. Be there right after dinner, and we'll show you who's the faster team," Justin said, trying to sound unruffled. His comic was twisted into such a tight roll he could have used it for a baseball bat.

Todd smiled and nodded sharply and dove back into the water.

Shawn sighed. "What if we get caught?" he asked, glancing consciously at Mike on the lifeguard stand. "My next junior counselor job depends on my experience here."

"We won't. We're better than that." Justin was certain now. "And if we beat these guys fairly maybe they'll leave us alone for the rest of camp." He noticed that his knee no longer hurt.

Shawn acquiesced with a shrug. "He is being an idiot about your Dad. If it's that important to you, man, count me in."

After a very quiet supper, Justin and Shawn repacked their backpacks from the morning circuit exercise and stealthily headed up to the trails. They had strategies planned for which trail to use and for a smooth exchange on the climb. Justin's knee was carefully rewrapped and his hiking boots securely laced. They were setting their watch timers when Todd and Steven arrived.

"All right we're good-to-go," Todd said briskly. Steven was looking around to be sure they were alone.

"Let's get this over with," Justin agreed. "And when we beat your times, you're gonna stay away from us for the rest of camp."

"Then you'd better get moving," Steven said, starting his timer and dashing toward their chosen trail.

Justin was thankful that Todd and Steven stayed true to form and chose the most challenging hiking trail. It was direct but full of obstacles; probably not somewhere inexperienced hikers should choose at the end of a long day of physical activity. Justin and Shawn's chosen trail had dried out, making it much easier to navigate. They had the advantage of reaching the climb zone first, which was helpful, as Todd and Steven were more experienced climbers. Shawn was fully harnessed and beginning his ascent when Todd and Steven arrived.

"What are you doing?" Shawn asked, incredulously, as Steven began to free climb the zone wearing only his helmet and gloves.

"I don't need safety gear for this little bouldering expedition," he called over, as he efficiently chose his holds and moved rapidly up the slope.

Shawn swore under his breath and paused briefly. He shook off his indecision and continued to ascend with full safety gear with Justin looking exasperated but still securing him at the base.

Justin tried his best to ignore Todd's constant stream of derogatory comments as they waited their turn. He concentrated on Shawn's smooth and speedy descent. Steven had a head start, but his descent was slower without rappelling. He still hit the base before Shawn, and Todd quickly moved forward to free climb the rock face without safety gear.

By then he'd had enough and blind anger took over reason. Justin was part-way up the climb without safety gear.

"Justin! Don't do it!" Shawn shouted. "It's not worth it!"

But Justin was in an unreachable zone. Todd was several meters away from him but still nattered comments like a persistent wasp throughout their climb (what was that about Mom?). Justin wanted to be rid of him once and for all. He pushed harder but somehow Todd's hand still slapped the taped marker before his.

Halfway down the slope Todd's path was close enough for Justin to hear him clearly. "Story of your life, huh, Attwood?"

Todd sneered.

He whipped his head around to reply and felt his foothold give way below him. He scrambled to regain his grip, but his focus was lost. Everything moved in agonizingly slow motion as he separated from the rock face. He cried out when his body rebounded off a large protruding boulder close to the base. His splayed landing was punctuated with a searing pain in his injured right knee. He thought Shawn was screaming but he sounded as if he were under water. Stinging tears filled his eyes as he rocked back and forth grasping his knee. Nothing he tried helped him escape the white-hot pain. Shawn finally broke through his pain by shaking his shoulders.

"Justin! Look at me! Hold still! I'm going to stabilize your leg and get you some help." Shawn looked around with the unlikely notion that Todd and Steven were still there to help. Of course, they instantly vanished down the trail. He propped Justin against his backpacks and headed toward the trail to find some materials to create a splint. Fortunately the mixed forest supplied plentiful resources, and he selected two straight, sturdy branches and another long, forked branch. Heading back toward the trail he gathered a remnant roll of surveyor tape used to mark the trails.

"Hang on, buddy, this is gonna hurt," he said to Justin, who was fighting back the urge to writhe in pain. Shawn straightened the leg as best he could, knowing he was successful when the growling sound Justin was making had stopped. He straddled Justin's leg, squeezing the branches firmly together with his knees while he securely wrapped the surveyor tape around his makeshift splint.

"OK?" Shawn asked.

Justin blinked rapidly and eventually nodded. The splint had actually relieved some of his immediate discomfort.

"Now, time to get up," Shawn said. He offered Justin the forked branch as a crutch. On the count of three they hauled themselves to standing. After several deep breaths Justin nodded to Shawn that he was ready to move.

Shawn took them down the tamest trail he remembered from the map. Eventually between the two boys and the crutch, they developed a rhythm moving down the hill that jostled between the need for speed and the need for pain control. Shawn talked constantly and breathlessly about any subject he could think of as they hobbled along. Justin appreciated that he wasn't required to reply.

A large boulder loomed near the last third of the trail. "Sit here," Shawn said. He propped Justin against the rock and handed him the water bottle from his pack. "I'm tired and so are you. I'm going to get Mike to help us get you to the nurse's station."

Again all Justin could do was nod. He stared at Shawn's feet as he deftly jogged his way down the trail. As the sound of his scrambling feet faded, the evening sounds of the forest enclosed Justin. The chattering squirrels and chirping crickets were soon drowned out by Justin's own thoughts.

What have I done? What if my knee is totally wrecked? We'll get kicked out for sure. Shawn doesn't deserve that. Why did I listen to Todd? Talk about an idiot.

His stomach churned as the impact of what happened settled in. He felt dizzy and clammy. He thought he might throw up. At least he forgot about his knee for a while. He breathed deeply to steady himself. After an eternity with his own thoughts he heard gravel crunching under fast footsteps.

Mike and Andrew flanked Shawn as they hurried up the trail.

With Justin's arms around their necks, Mike and Andrew supported him in a seated carry to the nurse's station.

"Gail! We've got a leg injury here," Mike yelled as they burst through the door. He and Andrew boosted Justin onto the exam table.

"You again?" nurse Gail said, rounding the corner with some ice packs. "Tell me what happened."

Shame burned in Justin's face as he related the whole embarrassing and painful story. As she carefully unstrapped the splint and iced the knee, Gail asked a few questions along the way to help her determine the extent of his injuries. Shawn supplied some answers but mostly he sat grimly on the moose-upholstered futon. Mike and Andrew listened intently, soaking up every detail.

Gail finished her assessment. "He'll need to go to the hospital to see the doctor and get x-rayed," she said as she applied the 'quick splint' to keep the knee immobilized. "By the way, nice work on the field dressing, Shawn," she added.

"I'll drive him," Mike said. "We'll give your parents a call from the hospital."

"Great," Gail said. She handed Justin a glass of water and two tablets. "I'll call ahead to let them know you're coming."

Justin jiggled the tablets in his hand. He wanted to say something to Shawn, but what? Downing the tablets, he watched his chance disappear as Andrew ushered Shawn out the door for a snack and some rest.

Next thing Justin knew he was loaded into Mike's roomy crew cab truck. It was only a fifteen minute ride to Glacier Springs, the small town in the foothills. But Justin felt a lifetime had passed in silence just driving out of the parking lot. Part way down the bumpy mountain trail, Justin couldn't take it any longer.

"Mike, I -," he started to say. But he couldn't find any words that justified his actions. The look on Mike's face was unreadable.

"The rules are in place for your safety, Justin," Mike said evenly. "I was certain that was something I didn't need to review with you and Shawn."

Justin closed his eyes and sighed in frustration. *I know that.* "I can't believe I let those guys get to me," he lamented. He felt that clammy feeling wash over him again.

Mike's tone softened. "I've attended camps and courses like this all my life. There are kids at every one of them who feel the need to prove themselves," he said. "It's hard to think about just doing your best and not worrying about anyone else - especially when some people are in your face all the time."

So Mike had seen what Todd and Steven were doing, Justin thought, surprised. His sick feeling eased a bit.

Mike seemed to read his thoughts. "But you still might not be able to finish camp. It depends on what the doctor says, your parents and the rest of the counselors," Mike said. "It also depends on what's important to you."

When they pulled up to the emergency room doors, a nurse was waiting with a wheelchair. She rolled Justin straight into the X-ray department. After another thorough examination, the doctor splinted his knee and tended his other scrapes and bruises from the fall. His X-rays showed no fractures, so Justin was advised to stay off his badly sprained knee for a few days, use his crutches and regularly take his medication.

He emerged from the treatment room feeling a bit like a mummy. He stiffly directed his crutches down the squeaky hospital floor. At the end of the hall he observed Mike talking on the pay phone. Better get this over with, he decided, willing his awkwardly-weighted body down the hallway.

Mike looked up as Justin slumped tiredly against the wall. "Thanks, Mr. Attwood. I'll hand you over to Justin," he said, passing the receiver over. He took a seat down the hall in the waiting area and began flipping through the magazines.

"Dad? Yeah, it's a bad sprain," Justin said quietly. "Tell Mom I'm really OK."

"Now I want you to tell me exactly what happened," Dad said. His voice was low and deep like a volcano about to explode.

Justin retold his story and decided it best not to leave any thing out. He had to make Dad understand. Maybe by being completely honest he could convince Dad that he wanted to stay at camp.

The end of his tale was marked by Dad's long pause on the other end. "You really challenged those boys?"

Justin was stunned. Not the comment he expected. A lecture about responsibility, maybe. Was Dad actually impressed? "Yeah, but I didn't set out to break the rules, Dad, but I was so sick of those guys' attitudes," Justin said. He was trying hard to control the emotion bubbling through his voice. "I just wanted to do camp stuff without them constantly riding me and Shawn. Please, Dad, I really want to stay – if they'll let me."

"You're sure your knee is going to be OK?" Dad asked.

"Doctor said taking it easy should make it as good as new," Justin answered. "Dad, I *will* take good care of it. And I promise to stay out of trouble. I know I can do it."

He paused. "All right, Jus, let me talk to Mike again," Dad said finally. "Make certain there are no more incidents and take care of that knee. Mom says to call if you need anything."

Justin felt like he just successfully jumped one hundred hurdles. "Thanks, Dad, I will," he said. He looked around for Mike and jumped in surprise to find him standing beside him. He gave Mike another turn with his Dad.

He was too tired to move, so he waited hopefully by the phone. Mike's final conversation with Dad consisted of a few short exchanges and ended on a note Justin could not interpret.

"We'll see what we can do, Mr. Attwood. Thanks. Bye."

Once loaded back into Mike's truck Justin still didn't have a chance to see if he would be staying at camp. He was asleep before Mike got behind the wheel.

CHAPTER 3

Justin tried to sit up comfortably in the nurse's station cot, but was painfully unsuccessful. Stiffness had settled in deeply overnight. Not that Justin remembered much after leaving the hospital. He awoke in Gail's observation room when the sunlight finally pierced through the heavy patterned drapes and found Shawn staring at him expectantly. From his spot in the canvas camping chair in the corner Shawn winced in sympathy at Justin's discomfort.

"It's just great that Dad thinks I can stay. But what if we get kicked out anyway?" Justin said. He groaned unwillingly as he strapped the foamy splint back on to his tightly bandaged leg. The doctor said he should wear it whenever possible during the day and especially when he was on his crutches.

"Didn't Mike say anything on the way back from the hospital?" Shawn asked.

"I don't remember. I fell asleep almost right after we left the hospital," Justin answered. "The doctor gave me some kind of shot, and I guess it knocked me flat."

Shawn shrugged and fiddled with the pocket on the leg of his shorts. He looked up as Nurse Gail appeared in the doorway with a couple of breakfast trays.

"Here you go, boys," she said as she set the trays on the side table. "I'll be back to check your leg when you're finished eating. Oh, and Mike will be right in to see you, if you're feeling up to a visitor."

"Sure," said Justin. He figured saying no to Mike's visit wasn't an option.

"Thanks for breakfast, Gail," Shawn added.

Gail smiled and disappeared as quickly as she had appeared. No sooner had she left then Mike's frame filled the doorway.

"Morning, boys. How's the knee?" Mike asked casually. He sat in a second canvas chair next to Justin's cot and leaned forward.

"It still hurts, but it's much better than last night," Justin said. He stared hard at his heavily bandaged knee. He still hadn't really apologized to Mike for his stupidity. If he couldn't explain himself to Mike how was he supposed to convince the rest of the instructors that he deserved to stay? He looked to Shawn for inspiration but he continued to re-button his short's pocket intensely.

Mike finally decided to relieve the boys of their misery. "After talking to your Dad and Shawn's mom, I talked to the other instructors on your behalf." Mike looked from one worried face to the other. "The decision was that you both can stay to finish camp, provided you follow the rules to the letter. And Justin, you must follow doctor's orders for treating your leg," Mike said.

The breath Shawn had been holding rushed out. "Thanks, Mike."

"I'll do whatever I need to," Justin said. "I really appreciate what you did, Mike."

"Well, all the instructors agreed you showed good skills and terrific teamwork during the exercises so far," Mike continued, "and how you handled yourselves after the accident was exceptional."

The news about being able to stay had renewed their zest for breakfast. But Mike's last comment halted their forks as Justin and Shawn exchanged confused glances. But Mike was still on a roll.

"If Justin heals well enough in the next couple of days you two will likely have enough practice days left to earn the skills and circuit times to participate in the camp final challenge," Mike said.

Both boys stopped chewing altogether and gaped openly at Mike. Justin remembered from the orientation session that there was a skill challenge during the last two days of camp that incorporated all the skills learned over the two weeks. The teams who qualified were assigned an instructor who helped them plan and execute a canoe, camping and hiking trip using the river that passed through Wapiti Junction. Justin couldn't believe after everything he'd done that he and Shawn would be considered for the challenge.

Mike simply shrugged. "So you made a bad decision, Justin. It happens even with experienced outdoorsmen," he explained. "It's what you do about your mistakes that counts."

Mike's jeans swished on the canvas chair as he rose to leave. He paused in the doorway. "And if you two can fly the straight and narrow path, I'll volunteer to be your instructor for the final challenge." He grinned and was gone.

"Wow," Shawn said, his fork still hovering over his plate.

"No kidding," Justin answered. He returned to his meal when he felt certain there were no more surprises in store for him at the moment.

Over the next two days Shawn and Justin spent their class time learning about orienteering, plant and animals. Justin was able to canoe, as long as he sat with his leg extended and propped on some extra lifejackets. When their section of campers went climbing, Shawn joined in. Justin was responsible for organizing and readying their harness equipment and handling the climbers' safety checklists. The message was not lost on him.

He was disappointed to discover that neither Todd nor Steven had been expelled from camp. He couldn't find out exactly what happened to them, but they were conspicuously absent from their section for the last few days. He did overhear Squirrel Girl – as he'd started thinking of her after she caught him tripping over the rodent on the first circuit –mention something about them.

She said she'd seen them helping the instructors teach fundamentals to the less experienced campers. Whatever was going on, it would make it hard for Todd and Steven to acquire enough skill points to qualify for the final challenge.

Although he couldn't hike the routes he and Shawn planned, Justine found he actually enjoyed the orienteering classes. He liked maps and found using a compass almost second nature. They would complete their assignments on paper, and then Shawn would test-hike the route with Justin giving feedback on a two-way radio. Justin could visualize the routes in his head and follow along easily from Shawn's descriptions. Shawn typically emerged from the forest exactly as planned in good time with a grin on his face.

Shawn thrived on the plants and animals class. "Too many *National Geographic* magazines," he said, chalking it up to all the ones he'd read waiting in his mom's office for her to finish work.

The plant stuff Justin could do without. He particularly liked the information about the large forest animals. Moose, black bears, grizzly bears, coyotes, lynx – where they lived, what they ate, what they thought of people – now that was cool.

One of the other instructors, Tim, was an excellent photographer and brought in his own pictures of everything they talked about. After hearing how most forest critters just wanted to mind their own business, Justin was fairly certain he never wanted to shoot a deer. Dad would just have to deal with Justin's space on the trophy wall being unfilled. Now Justin had to find the words to explain that to him.

During classes Justin took no chances and treated his knee with kid gloves. Nearing the end of the week, he was well on his way to being fully healed. After classes on Wednesday, He sat expectantly in Gail's treatment room.

"Take a few steps – slowly," she said, having removed all his bandages and reexamined his knee. She helped him to stand and stood close by while he made his attempt.

Gingerly Justin put some weight on his tender knee. Not so bad, he thought. He took a short, hopping step and found the leg to be a bit uncooperative. Instinctively he clasped Gail's shoulder.

"Sorry. It feels weird. Not painful, but more like when you get back on skates the first time each winter," Justin said.

Gail laughed. "That's probably a good sign. I want you to take short practices on it a few times each day. Keep the splint on otherwise, and I'll check it again on Friday."

Friday. That was the day when teams would be selected to prepare for the final challenge. He and Shawn had done everything possible to not wreck their chances at qualifying.

Yet Friday afternoon came quicker than Justin would have guessed. His knee had been cooperating nicely and hiss trial runs over the past two days only left him with minor stiffness. He could put all his weight on it and almost walk with a normal gait. He wasn't sure the knee's endurance would last a whole day of physical activity yet, so he was cautious to follow Gail's recommendations.

At the moment his knee was propped comfortably on his backpack, and he whistled while stowing the climbing gear.

The rest of his section was getting debriefed on today's climb. Todd and Steven were back but they seemed like the wind was taken out of their sails. Justin almost didn't pay any attention to them whatsoever.

He had finished sorting the gear into the various storage tubs when he saw Mike and Shawn heading toward him. His stomach did a nervous flip.

"You're in, boys," Mike said, smiling. He gave both boys a congratulatory clap on their shoulders. "You'd better get a good night's sleep because we're meeting tomorrow morning before classes start to begin planning our trip." He helped Justin stack the storage tubs. "We'll work again after dinner and again on Sunday. Hope you're up for the extra hours."

"All right!" Justin whooped, giving Shawn a high-five.

"Now let's get some dinner. I'm starving," Mike said. He handed Justin his crutches for getting down the hill. "We need that knee in top shape!"

All the preparation for the final challenge was completed above and beyond regular camp instruction. The challenge consisted of planning and mapping a river route to a designated campsite, then setting up an overnight camp.

In the morning, the team would navigate its way on foot back to the starting point on the river. Each team would choose different starting points, but their assigned instructors would see that the overall distance traveled would be equal and address all required skills. Other campers not in the challenge would take a river trip later to do a deep woods hike and collect the canoes left behind at the overnight campsites.

Justin found himself rolling the maps and plans for the challenge in his mind in every free moment. Mike was a great resource, and he conversed easily with the boys while they worked. Justin was amazed to discover that Mike was actually a graduate student in environmental studies at the northern university. In his spare time, which there was little of between classes, field exercises and research, Mike worked part-time as a park ranger for Forestry Services. Before this, it never occurred to Justin that Mike had a life outside of being an instructor at Wapiti Junction.

Shawn was just as interested. When he had the chance, he peppered Mike with questions about classes at university that dealt with plants and animals. *Totally brainwashed by National Geographic*, Justin smiled to himself. Needless to say, Mike offered their team substantial field experience upon which to draw. If Mike was this skilled, what were the other instructors like? What resources did the other teams have at their disposal?

But Mike always left the final decisions up to Justin and Shawn. "I planned enough of these in my years at camp and at school. This is your trip. I'm just here to offer suggestions and make sure it's do-able," he said.

Luckily Shawn had a keen eye for evaluating what gear was and wasn't required for the trip they planned. He diligently maintained a list of necessities versus possibilities, and corresponding piles of kit were growing in their cabin. Ultimately all they needed had to boil down into three backpacks they could lift and fit into the canoe.

"Maybe we could just boil tree bark for soup instead of bringing along ingredients," Shawn joked, after a recent attempt to reduce the volume of their gear.

"That's about how good my cooking tastes anyway," Justin answered, "so you wouldn't know the difference."

Even though the boys seemed to be working double time, Justin was sure he was enjoying himself more. His knee was fully functional by early the second week, but he still rested it when he had the chance. He was glad to be able to hike again, but Gail recommended that he not climb. This didn't exactly break his heart. Climbing didn't thrill him as much after his accident.

He invested his spare moments wisely in reviewing their maps and plans. Mike had suggested they also think of contingency plans, such as what they'd do if their camp spot were occupied by a bear or if rain soaked the site. Shawn continued to re-evaluate the gear. He packed and repacked it several times, checking it against his list of needs until he was satisfied they were set.

On Thursday all the challenge teams were excused from regular classes to complete their final checks. Justin and Shawn met Mike at the boathouse to haul their canoe to their chosen entry point along the river. As they boosted the canoe over their heads, it occurred to Justin that theirs was the farthest entry point away from camp. When they planned this he hadn't considered portaging the canoe across the distance.

"Hope I have enough energy to paddle," Shawn said.

Justin knew he enjoyed teasing him. "Yeah, yeah, yeah," he answered, gritting his teeth and readjusting the canoe's position on his shoulders. The canoe was beginning to feel like it was made of lead.

When they finally reached the entry point, they were all breathing heavily. *Thank goodness we brought the packs down here first*, Justin thought. Some time paddling on the cool river would be great.

They successfully lowered the canoe partly in the water and balanced the pack in the middle. Shawn would man the bow and

Justin would steer. Mike determined he got to sit in the center and enjoy the ride, as age should have its privileges.

"I'll also make sure the packs don't jump overboard," he said with mock seriousness. "At least you guys won't have to spend energy worrying about that."

Amazingly, the canoe still floated when filled with three packs and three tall guys. A few practice strokes up the river they settled into a paddling rhythm that moved them smoothly through the water. They rounded an easy bend when Shawn stopped paddling.

"My toes are wet."

Mike shifted his legs. "The packs are damp, too. We must have a slow leak."

"Turning for shore," Justin said. He felt a surge of frustration. They had checked everything more than once.

As the examined the overturned canoe on shore, Justin had an irrational thought: Todd and Steven. *What if they got to our stuff and sabotaged it? They've got to be angry that we got the challenge and they didn't. Don't be ridiculous*, he sharply told himself, *the boathouse is always locked, and these things happen.* He shook off his old uncertainties and concentrated on the canoe.

"Here it is. A small slice in the fiberglass," Mike said. "Definitely would allow seeping." He paused to consider their options. "This is the only canoe of this size. If we get one of the smaller ones we'll have to scale our gear down again. So we're better off patching it. But it shouldn't be a problem."

They loaded up their packs to return to camp for a patch kit. Shawn gave his pack one last heft onto his back and heard a strap snap.

"Oh, man!" said Shawn. He nearly lost his balance as the pack swung free of his left shoulder. Fortunately only one clasp was broken. "Well, this is the only large pack I brought. But I bet I can tie it together well enough to make the trip," Shawn said, checking the rest of the straps. "Guess I shouldn't stuff any more gear in here."

Mike nodded, and Justin frowned. *Trust Shawn to see the bright side of things. But we just don't need any more equipment failure right now.*

But Mike didn't seem overly concerned. After dropping their packs at camp, they scrounged a patch kit from the boathouse and walked back to the canoe. The patching went smoothly, and the canoe was left to dry. They stowed the paddles and lifejackets underneath it in case it rained over night. A river trip in an already-soggy lifejacket would be unnecessarily unpleasant.

In the main hall, Mike rigged Shawn's backpack. Mike noticed the concern that had ingrained itself across Justin's face. "Don't worry, Justin. The canoe is fine. With that patch it will be able to handle even the fastest water in the river," he said. "As for this pack, all the knot-tying I learned in scouts won't be wasted."

With all the preparations under control by late afternoon, Shawn and Justin enthusiastically headed to the Blue Moose. A good dinner followed by hot chocolate around the campfire improved Justin's mood. Later in their cabin, took time to stuff their clothes pockets with the essential materials.

"Here. We'll each take a waterproof match container. And I'll keep the small first aid kit in my leg pocket," Shawn said. He tossed Justin the match container and a couple of granola bars.

Justin zipped his maps and a marker into a sealed plastic bag. "I'll keep this in my shirt pocket with my compass."

"And don't' forget your Swiss Army knife," Shawn added, sliding his into his pants pocket. He tugged hard on his reinforced pack strap and surveyed his packing with a satisfied smile. "Now all that's left is a good night's sleep."

"You can sleep no matter what," Justin said. He tried to slide his hiking boot off but the lace was caught in the top hook. He jerked the boot to free it but the laced snapped.

"Great. More busted gear."

"Man, don't worry about it. Laces and straps break. Canoes leak. We'll still have an awesome trip," Shawn reassured him, tossing over a new bootlace from his bag.

"Yeah, I guess you're right."

Shawn was asleep before Justin had laced his boot. Once in his cot, he flipped around until he was as cozy as possible. But sleep eluded him for many long minutes. Finally his weary body overtook his busy head, and he didn't stir until the alarm clock hollered at him.

Justin's misgivings from the previous night were whisked away. The bacon and pancakes for breakfast were delicious; although, given how much he ate, he prayed he would fall overboard or he'd sink for sure. The canoe looked perfectly sealed, and the lifejackets were dry. Shawn's pack was securely strapped to his back, making Justin wonder vaguely if he should have had Mike knot the straps on his backpack, too. They quickly readied the canoe and loaded it for launch.

Each team's launch time was staggered to avoid any chances of congestion along the river. Justin's team had their canoe launched promptly at nine o'clock.

The day was overcast but the Windermere River was wide and calm. They quickly found the paddling rhythm they achieved in practice, and soon the surrounding forest whizzed past. It reminded Justin of how the tree line looked along the mountain road as he drove up to camp with Dad. However, with Mike and Shawn's company, this had the makings of a much more enjoyable trip. They comfortably lapsed in and out of conversations as they paddled. When they were quiet, Justin heard only the paddles dipping into the river and the animals of the forest creating the cacophony of their daily business.

As they wound their way up the ever-changing river, Justin began to believe the troubles that plagued their preparations had washed downriver like shed leaves. He relaxed into his paddling and started hunting for animals at the forest edge.

They were about halfway into their river course when a gain in the water speed brought his attention back to the canoe.

"We're picking up speed," Mike called over his shoulder to Justin.

"A lot rougher, too," Justin yelled so Shawn could hear. He firmed up his grip on his paddle and readied himself to dig in. When he'd consulted the maps to plan this trip he'd noted the water was described as faster in this part of the Windermere.

He didn't expect it to be quite this fast. The nature of the river had morphed into narrow shores, some whitewater flowing over irregular terrain and places where he could no longer see the bottom. He could see the tension in Shawn's shoulders as he paddled and scanned the path ahead for signs of sudden change.

What happened next took a split second. Justin's paddle sucked into the snaking river. The canoe lurched forward violently.

Mike and Shawn yelled simultaneously. Justin tried to recover control of the canoe. His paddle flayed wildly.

Mike shifted his weight to regain balance as Shawn struggled with his paddle. Mike screamed out some instructions that were drowned out by an ear-splitting crack.

The canoe slammed and shattered against an enormous boulder. Justin blasted through the water with such force it knocked the wind out of him. Bursting through the raging water, he gulped air and lunged for a large piece of the canoe as it swirled into his sight.

Justin whipped his head around in every direction. *Where were Mike and Shawn?*

He could see only wreckage.

CHAPTER 4

Kick harder. Stay above water. Look for Shawn and Mike.

Despite the upward push of his lifejacket, Justin's legs scrambled furiously against the dragging undertow. Searching wildly, he shoved heavy water in all directions. He sighted only a sheared paddle that eddied into his reach. Other than his chunk of canoe, it was the only piece of wreckage he had seen. The only *anything* he'd seen. He grabbed the paddle before it jammed into his shoulder. Supporting his body on his two salvaged pieces, he scanned the river one last time.

They've drowned. And I'm alone.

The sickening feeling was filling the pit of Justin's stomach when Shawn exploded through the river's surface. Justin's heart both soared and sank in seconds as Shawn's head dunked back beneath the water.

Justin held his breath in fear. Then the water broke a second time as Shawn managed to thrust Mike's head and shoulders above the surface.

"Help!" Shawn sputtered.

In late summer, the temperature of the river was cold enough to dull Justin's muscles. Steering his canoe pieces toward Shawn, Justin willed his body forward against the buoyancy of his lifejacket. He moved slowly as if treading quicksand. With great effort he shoved the broken paddle to Shawn. Moving his arms against their numbness, he struggled to help Shawn boost Mike's sagging body over the canoe paddle.

"We have to get to shore," Shawn said through chattering teeth.

Navigating three bodies through dangerous water was slow going. They jerked toward shore by alternating kicks and pushes off larger rocks. With every few kicks, Mike needed repositioning on the paddle as his lifejacket threatened to move him in the wrong direction.

"A couple more kicks, Shawn," Justin yelled over the rush of water. "I feel bottom!"

He dug his feet deeper into the silty river bottom, but the sand slipped away. Closer to shore the sand base was packed more firmly. But the slick, worn rocks offered more poor footing. At least the river itself became more shallow and slower near the edge.

Shawn and Justin heaved themselves toward shore with Mike in tow. They thrust his lead-weighted form as far onto the ragged edge as they could. With Mike safely on shore, they slumped in exhaustion on the moist earth.

Justin panted heavily as if his lungs might never be full of air again. His heart hammered against his chest wall louder than the background river rush. Out the corner of his eye, Justin saw Shawn fairing no better. Shawn stared skyward, his body motionless except for his heaving chest.

So when Shawn spoke suddenly, Justin nearly jumped out of his icy cold skin.

"We have to help Mike. He's really hurt," Shawn said, breathlessly.

Both boys forced themselves to stand and face their situation. As Justin looked beyond the river's edge, he realized how grateful he was to be out of the water alive.

We all could have died.

The adrenalin rush that swept his body threatened to drop him to his knees, but he willed himself to the task of helping Mike.

Fear gripped Justin as he wondered if Mike really was alive. Shuddering, he quickly shoved the creepy feeling away. He focused on helping Shawn move Mike to a safer place.

Mike just HAS to be alive. At least Shawn's acting like he is, so that's something.

While the boys adjusted their positions to safely lift their instructor, Justin risked a closer look at Mike's condition. An angry purple bruise shaded his right temple and most of his forehead. Several ragged cuts streaked Mike's arms between the shreds of his shirtsleeves.

He must have slammed into those big rocks like the canoe did.

Justin then concentrated on Mike's lifejacket, hoping to see it rise and fall with Mike's breathing. Five seconds. Ten seconds. Nothing.

"Ready – lift!" Shawn said, snapping Justin back to the task at hand.

Not far from the river's edge the fringes of tree line began. Justin's eyes focused on a grassy area under a cover of poplar trees that seemed safe enough.

"Let's get him over there."

Again they struggled to move Mike's body, but this time their effort wasn't wasted against the river's powerful currents. They maneuvered Mike into a sitting position to strip off his drenched lifejacket, then onto his back using his lifejacket as a pillow. Shawn gently adjusted Mike's head and shoulders into a more comfortable position. He leaned his ear toward Mike's mouth and carefully studied his chest.

"He's breathing. But that leg doesn't look good."

Justin followed Shawn's gaze down to Mike's lower left leg.

He couldn't tear his eyes away from what he saw. *What was that thing stuck in Mike's leg? A tree branch must have gotten wedged in his pant leg when we dragged him over here.*

"Not good," Shawn said seriously, piercing Justin's stunned thoughts. "His leg is broken, and he's losing blood where the bone broke through the skin."

Broken bone. Broken skin. Blood loss. A wave of nausea made Justin stagger over to a poplar for support. Deep breaths helped him rally before Shawn started talking again.

"We need to stop the bleeding with something."

With a task to do, the nausea eased. Justin hurried back to the shoreline to see if any of their gear survived the wreck. He saw only water and rocks and bits of forest debris swirling on the bubbling surface. The river acted as if nothing had disturbed it.

"Everything is gone," Justin reported back to Shawn. "So all we have is what we've got with us."

Both boys paused silently, considering their plight. Then grim resolve hit them.

Justin dug out the knife that was safely zipped into his cargo pants' pocket. He peeled off his soggy lifejacket and shredded strips from his shirt. He wrung out his freshly-made bandage strips, draped them over his arm and waited for Shawn.

Producing his own safely-stowed knife, Shawn dug up chunks of spongy moss and piled them next to Mike's leg. He wiped the knife clean, and used it to pick the bloody, shredded pant edges away from Mike's injury. Shawn carefully exposed the jagged wound, and did his best to clear out small bits of debris. He surrounded the protruding bone with the moss, pressing down firmly to stop the seeping blood. Fighting off another wave of nausea, Justin passed Shawn the shirt strips to secure the moss padding.

Shawn knelt back to examine his work. "Now the bleeding should slow, and no more dirt will get in it. But we still need to lift his legs so he doesn't go into shock."

Justin had a vague idea what shock was from watching doctor shows on television. He wished that he'd taken that first aid course at the YMCA last winter.

I'd be more useful to Mike and Shawn now.

But necessity kick-started his brain. He found four same-sized rocks to form a square under Mike's legs. He grabbed his lifejacket to pad the rocks and motioned to Shawn to add his to the pile. The bandage held firm as the boys carefully arranged Mike's legs on the prop.

Shawn nodded. "Pretty good, for what we've got," he said, teeth chattering again. He cupped his hands and blew into them. "I'm freezing. We need a fire. Mostly, Mike needs a fire."

Again Justin was grateful for their planning. He fished his waterproof match case out of his pants pocket and held it up like a trophy. "Ta da!"

Shawn mustered a grin for their small victory and scrambled to his feet. "And we have lots of firewood."

They trekked farther back into the trees to gather dry deadfall. They stacked their firewood into a rock-enclosed spot they created not far away from Mike's body. Once they tindered the branch pile with fallen dry leaves, Justin produced one precious match to ignite the fire.

"Here we go."

Shawn didn't move a muscle while Justin swiped the match near the branches. Justin allowed the small flame to slowly lick the dry leaves in several places. He blew gently into his creation and waited patiently. Only when the larger branches flared did Justin consider himself successful.

They stacked the fire with more deadfall until they were sure it wouldn't burn out quickly. They removed their soaking shirts, boots and socks, propping them near the fire to dry. Wearily both boys sat down cross-legged by the fire in hopes of warming and drying the rest of themselves. They poked quietly at the fire with forked branches, mesmerized by the flames. Finally Shawn spoke.

"So, everything's gone?"

Justin kept stabbing at the fire and nodded. "No radios, no tent, no food – no frills," he said with a touch of humor that made Shawn smile slightly. "Nothing but what we packed on ourselves."

Shawn swallowed hard. "Well, let's see what we've got."

They fished around in all their pockets and deposited their meager gear onto the ground – two waterproof match cases, two Swiss Army knives, four granola bars, a compass, a small LED flashlight, their wristwatches, Shawn's spare first-aid-kit-in-a baggy, and Justin's basic map and marker sealed in a zippered plastic bag.

"Better than nothing," Shawn said.

Justin marveled at the way Shawn was always able to make lemonade out of lemons. But they had bigger problems than just limited gear.

"The real trouble is no one's going to miss us until late tomorrow. And since we're the ones farthest upstream, it's not like anyone's going to come past here," Justin said.

Shawn frowned and surveyed Mike's still-unmoving frame. "He's not doing well. He hasn't woken up. His leg is still losing blood, and I'm not sure if he's hurt anywhere else. And even though our fire's great, it's going to get colder overnight."

Justin paused to soak this in. "So what you're saying is that one of us needs to go for help."

Shawn nodded grimly.

Justin tore open the zippered bag and unfolded his map. He studied the basic map markers he'd plotted from Wapiti Junction's master maps. He checked his watch. "The best I can figure is that we're about here." He pointed to a section of the river course that curved much like the last part they paddled through before the crash. "The nearest park ranger station is upstream, heading farther up the mountain base. Give or take a few twists, the river flows right past the station. The land around it just gets steeper and rockier."

"How long would it take?" Shawn asked, still eyeing Mike's injury.

"About another fifteen kilometers - uphill," Justin answered. His head was really working now. *Could I do this?*

"I'll flip you for it," Shawn said. His knit eyebrows hinted his concern.

"Not this time, Shawn," Justin said. His mind was made up. He knew what he had to do. "With your first aid training, Mike needs you."

Shawn protested. "But what about your sprained knee?"

Justin hadn't even considered his previous injury. It seemed like nothing compared to all this.

"It's fine right now, and it will just have to stay that way," Justin said firmly. "I studied the maps in detail back at camp. I'm the one who can get to the ranger station."

CHAPTER 5

I have to make it. I can make it. I will make it.

The mantra ran repeatedly through his head to the odd rhythm of his footsteps over the uneven terrain. His hands occasionally felt his semi-dry pockets to make sure his limited gear was still in place. His shoes and socks were not completely dry, but he couldn't wait by the fire any longer before leaving. His shirt, or rather, Shawn's shirt, was the driest piece of clothing he wore.

"I'll wear your ripped one," Shawn had reasoned while they loaded Justin's gear for his trek. "You'll need all the body cover you can get when it gets colder."

How much colder? Justin resolved to not worry about this right now, but he still couldn't help wishing for a jacket. Mom always said to take a jacket with him just in case he needed it. He pulled his thoughts away from home, and began mentally reciting his mantra again.

If his situation hadn't been so desperate, he would have thought the scenery was beautiful. Evergreen and poplar trees mingled with rocks jutted against the early evening sky. He breathed the mixed scents of pine needles and fresh-fallen leaves that carpeted the ground. As the sun sunk, the sounds of nature grew louder as the forest creatures prepared for night.

On cue for suppertime, Justin's stomach growled. He'd walked about an hour and wasn't surprised when his body reminded him about how little he'd eaten for the day.

A plateful of the Blue Moose's macaroni and cheese would be great. He settled for chunks from one of his precious granola bars. Savoring the first bite to make it last, he tucked the rest of the bar securely back into his shirt pocket.

Chewing slowly, Justin took the time to check his compass and note what landmarks he could on his makeshift map. He felt sure he was well on track and could retrace his path for the search and rescue team. The river itself guided him as he loosely followed its course upstream toward the ranger station.

Justin chose safer, more direct footing through the trees when the river's shoreline gradually became more sloped and rocky the farther he hiked. As long as he could hear the water's roar he figured he was doing fine.

A crisp breeze funneled around where he stood, swirling up loose leaves and snaking a chill up his back. He glanced skyward at the swaying treetops and windswept clouds. A few more hours left before sunset, so he'd better get moving. Not far off gathering rain clouds warned of even earlier darkness. He tucked his map back into the safety of its plastic bag.

Great. Soon I'll be cold, hungry and even wetter. He stepped forward but was halted by a painful twinge shooting up his right knee.

"Ow!" he yelled, crouching down to rub his old injury. The echo of his yell hung in the air as he massaged his knee. The loudness of his own voice surprised him, and he looked around nervously. He shook off the strange feeling that he had somehow intruded on the forest's solitude. *Not like anyone can hear me. What's that saying about nobody hearing a tree fall in the forest?*

Rising slowly, Justin gingerly tested his knee. No more twinges threatened his ability to hike. He breathed a sigh of relief and moved on cautiously. *I guess that's why Nurse Gail said to take it easy. Must have stressed my knee kicking in the river and now all this hiking. Well, it just can't give out yet.*

His knee loosened with each careful step. The journey was long enough without his knee working properly. He tried to continue his walking mantra, but worries about his troublesome knee and unfulfilled stomach directed his thoughts back home.

Mom would be cooking dinner right now. Roast beef and Yorkshire pudding. That would be even better than macaroni and cheese. He suddenly wished he could talk to her. A strange pang clutched his heart. Was that homesickness?

Keep going, Jus, your friends need you. That's what she'd say if she was here. *Trust yourself. You have good instincts if you'd just listen to them.* Justin smiled at a clear memory of him and Mom chatting over cups of hot chocolate after a rough hockey practice that almost made him quit. He remembered Dad jumping in to say that Justin just needed to be more aggressive so his teammates would respect him. Dad never did understand his point of view. What would Dad say about this situation?

He'd probably jump to the conclusion that the canoe capsize was my fault. Like I wasn't paddling hard enough. That thought stopped

Justin in his tracks. He gazed into the maze of pine trees ahead and visualized the whole crash again.

Was it my fault? No, no, his instincts told him. Shawn and Mike were taken off guard and couldn't recover the canoe either. Nobody was at fault. The canoe capsize was an accident. Sometimes you can't fight Mother Nature no matter how well prepared you are.

With that one worry resolved, he quickly pressed on wondering how he got from hot chocolate to the crash being his fault.

Everything and everyone is connected. Justin remembered learning something about that in Social Studies class last semester. Now he was connected to Mike and Shawn, and he could not fail to get to the ranger station. With new resolve Justin was again able to hike to the rhythm of his mantra.

But, as usual, Justin's luck was never able to hold for long. The rain drizzled down shortly after he began making good time over more even ground. He seemed to get rained on twice, as the water that didn't fall on him directly from the ominous navy clouds funneled down the pine branches and doused him again.

He remembered wishing for a jacket, but now he'd have settled for a cap to shield his eyes. The smooth, flat terrain that gained him time and distance before the rain now offered him a slick surface worse than black ice on a winter highway. Every few steps his boots slid out from under him, leaving him fumbling for support from overhanging tree branches. As the branches slung low from his weight, they deposited more rainwater onto him.

Feeling frustrated with his slow progress, Justin stopped under a thick pine canopy to recheck his route. Unfortunately, his map was of little help. There was nothing really wrong with his chosen route except that it wasn't fast enough when rain-soaked. He decided to scout a path closer to the river's edge. Following the river's winding path would probably take longer, but closer to shore might be easier to hike. Ducking branches and thrashing through low-lying shrubs, Justin discovered a deer trail sloping down to the river.

Perfect. *All animals need to drink. Even with this rain I could use some water.* Justin cautiously worked his way down the trail. Clearly hooves were better suited to this moss-covered trail than soggy hiking boots. Again Justin grabbed at what branches he could catch to slow his descent. Seeing the trail begin to level out, he attempted to skid down the rest of the way. Two meters from the end of the slope his right boot heel snagged a half-buried tree root. Justin's feet swooped from the ground moments before his shoulder smashed onto the trail.

Instinctively, he flowed with the motion, tucking and rolling to the bottom. He finished his tumble splayed out ungracefully on his back on level ground. He lay still for some time, testing each body part for injury. His right knee had been jarred again, but luckily no sharp pain greeted his probing movements. He sucked in a deep, cleansing breath after determining he was not seriously injured.

But I'm going to ache all over later, especially my poor knee. He stood slowly, favoring his knee and checking his arms and legs for cuts and bruises on the way up. Only a few minor scrapes marked his limbs underneath the caked-on dirt and wet pine needles. Some of the pine needles stuck straight out from his knees and elbows, making Justin look like a porcupine.

Justin smiled to himself and wished one of his buddies were here to videotape his epic wipeout like they did when they went mountain biking. He was sure none of the guys had body-surfed down a mountain trail before.

And I bet none of the deer come down like that either. He brushed the forest matter from his clothes, pleased that he had survived yet another of nature's challenges. Finally Justin raised his head to survey his surroundings.

The rumbling snort made him freeze instantly. Justin's gaze locked onto the bull moose standing belly-deep in the river several meters away.

Just great.

CHAPTER 6

The moose stared curiously through the drizzling rain in Justin's direction, methodically chewing the plants that hung from each side of his horse-like mouth. Justin rifled quickly through the information in his head about what he'd learned in camp's native species classes.

He may not have been as enthusiastic as Shawn was about all the plants, but he paid closer attention when Tim, the instructor, talked about large animals. Maybe if he'd read a few more of Shawn's *National Geographic* magazines this information would come back more quickly. He stood as a statue, imagining the amazing photographs Tim showed in class. There was one picture that looked just like this moose did now – standing up to its furry brown belly in river water. Justin breathed a quiet sigh of relief as some of the moose-facts he'd learned began trickling back to him.

He was quite sure the moose didn't see him very well, as moose weren't as sharp-eyed as other forest creatures. They didn't need to be: hardly anything ever attacked them. Tim told one story about a moose fending off an entire wolf pack using just its hooves and antlers. At the time Justin had pictured a cartoon-style moose flinging one yelping wolf after another far into the forest. Face-to-face with a full-grown male moose, he realistically understood the wolves would stand little chance. The moose's antler span was nearly as wide as Justin was tall, with each velvety antler adorned with a mix of heavy, flat paddles and pointy tines.

The moose continued to chew steadily while staring in Justin's direction. Justin remained rigid, unsure what his next move should be. Beside his amazement with the moose's stunning antlers, he was fascinated by the rest of the moose's awkward features – the equine, sloping nose and heavily-muscled body perched on gangly legs. But he knew from class this animal was definitely not awkward in its environment. Justin wished he were as well suited to this habitat. Then he might not be having so much difficulty moving upstream.

The moose took another mouthful of plants from the river and continued watching Justin. He wondered what kind of animal the moose thought he was. Justin recalled laughing at another story Tim told about a moose that chased a Jeep bound for work each morning for a week during mating season, probably thinking it was another moose. *I hope he doesn't get the same idea.*

Funny as that thought was, the real problem was that the presence of this moose was wasting Justin's precious time. He getting no closer to the ranger station and images of Shawn and Mike spurred him to make a move. Keeping his eyes fixed on the moose, he slowly stepped backward.

He'd retreated two steps when he noticed the ruffled hair on the moose's broad neck stand up straight. The moose's large ears pinned tightly against his head. Justin's heart nearly leapt out of his chest as the moose thrust himself forward with such force that water whirl pooled loudly around his powerful legs. The moose planted himself solidly in the swirling water with antlers tilted in Justin's direction.

Clearly the moose took walking backwards to mean something other than what Justin intended. Justin stopped dead in his tracks.

Uh oh.

Justin's heart raced through several moments of panic. He struggled to gain control over his rapid breathing in case the moose should find this offensive as well. Luckily the huge animal also halted after wading back a few steps. The moose's movement stirred the water, releasing a smell that reminded Justin of his Granddad's musty cellar where he stored his garden-grown vegetables each year. The bull moose must have dined in a very tasty marsh recently and carried the swamp scent in his thick coat to the river. The pungent scent rallied Justin's attention, allowing him to focus on the situation at hand. He immediately resumed his safe statue pose, and closely watched the moose's behavior.

I guess I'll have to wait him out a bit longer.

He thought more about what Tim had said about moose in class, hoping to come up with another option for escaping. Justin figured he couldn't outrun the moose because Tim said they could sprint for short bursts. If the moose caught him, he'd likely be trampled by four pancake-sized hooves. He'd be less successful in the water as the moose could easily out-swim him.

Well, no running and no swimming. That leaves flying, and I'll probably not sprout wings any time soon.

Without any obvious solution to his present problem, Justin returned to monitoring the moose. Soon fatigue and the waiting game with the persistent creature made Justin's mind wander. He mentally shook his head about the ridiculousness of his stalemate. *What would my friends say if they could see me right now? How would*

I explain it to Mike and Shawn that I couldn't get through because of a standoff with a moose?

He tried not to think about what was happening to Mike and Shawn. Worrying about them gave him a sick, desperate feeling that made it harder to keep going. Using the ranger station as the target for his 'mission' rather than the idea of helping his friends stowed his worry in a safer place.

Dad would call this weakness – not being able to put your feelings completely aside to get the job done. It always came down to Dad wanting Justin to be more assertive. Go out there and grab hold of what you want. Be more like Jason. Be more like Dad.

That was the problem. Whatever the goal, it wasn't usually what Justin wanted, but what Dad wanted. His brother, Jason, never seemed to struggle with Dad's ideals, so why was it so challenging for Justin? He supposed different things mattered to him. Mom usually understood that. She mostly wanted Justin to do the things he enjoyed and always try his best, no matter how things turned out. Mom favored skill and sportsmanship over assertiveness.

Then it hit him. Maybe that's the approach he needed with this moose! *I have to change my actions with him or it will be dark, and I'll still be stuck in this staring contest.*

With the combined dimness of evening, heavy rain clouds and the moose's poor eyesight, Justin thought he might be able to fool the moose. Without shifting his feet he began to crouch in super-slow motion. These movements mattered little to the moose, who kept chewing and watching.

Reaching toward the ground, he felt around for a good-sized rock. Justin padded his hand along the shore without taking his eyes of the moose. Having no luck with his right hand, he slowly extended his left for another ground sweep. At last his fingers nicked a heavier rock just beyond easy reach. He stretched, praying he wouldn't fall over, and rolled the palm-sized rock into his grasp.

His thigh muscles burned as he pushed through his slow motion ascent. Once standing, he smoothly traded the rock to his right hand.

Still the moose chewed and watched, undisturbed by Justin's up and down movements. *Maybe only walking backwards makes him mad.*

Justin only had to wait a few moments for his opportunity. As the moose dunked his head under water for another bite, Justin launched his rock with perfect timing to when the moose raised his enormous head. Justin quickly assumed the statue pose before the moose realized anything had happened. Seconds later the rock plopped loudly in the river behind the moose.

With speed that Justin would not have believed possible, the moose swung his huge body to face the disruptive sound. Justin sprung as noiselessly as he could back up the deer trail. He zigzagged into the surrounding brush and hunkered down to hide himself from the moose's view. Through the dripping branches he watched the moose pondering the new noise.

Only moments passed before the moose lost interest in the river altogether and waded onto the opposite shore. Soon the dark brown animal was completely concealed by the forest.

Justin let out the breath he'd been holding and sank to the ground to rest his tired legs. He fished around his pocket for the rest of his granola bar. He enjoyed his well-deserved snack while watching the moose's exit point to be sure he wouldn't return.

He stuffed the wrapper back into his pocket and glanced at his watch – just after eight o'clock. Justin groaned at the time he'd lost because of the moose encounter and heaved himself off the damp ground. Armed with his new experience with the forest and one of its creatures, he successfully descended the deer trail without wiping out and took the chance to get his much-needed drink of water. Keeping to 'his' side of the river he set out with renewed determination to make up valuable lost time.

CHAPTER 7

Traveling the shoreline was only marginally better than hiking through the dense forest. Once past the slower, wider part where the moose had entered, the Windermere curved and twisted and picked up speed. Faster water was paired with a rockier shore, creating poor footing near the edge. Farther upstream the shoreline almost vanished as the rocks peppered the steep slope all the way to the treeline. Justin had no choice except to head back to higher ground.

The rain had eased slightly, helping Justin see his path more clearly. He knew this improved visibility would be short-lived as twilight settled into the forest. The light shower kept the rocks slippery and treacherous, especially under drenched hiking boots.

Justin felt like a baby mountain goat on his hooves for the first time. He had many starts and stops as he picked his path up the slope. More than once he stumbled and raked his bare legs into the jagged rocks. Each time he twisted his body to avoid jamming his vulnerable right knee. Impending darkness and the time lost to the moose forced him past the discomfort of his growing collection of scrapes and bruises.

Breathless and weary, he finally hauled his body safely over the upper ledge. *Back in the forest again.* But this time he was grateful for the partial shelter offered by the canopy of branches. Justin settled under a thick overhang of intertwined branches tight enough to keep most of the rain off.

He checked his compass and was happy he was oriented in the necessary direction. He then pulled out his map and added the details about the river's winding course from memory. He hadn't added anything to the map since before he'd encountered the moose. He'd concentrated only on covering distance and making up lost time while he could along the shoreline.

But the rock climb back to the treeline had sucked away more precious minutes and left his tender knee feeling stiff and sore. Pressing the side light button on his watch, he risked a glance at the time. After losing so much time with the moose, he felt he was racing against sunset to get help. So he tried not to constantly look at the time, because it just made him more anxious when things weren't going smoothly.

He concentrated only on covering the distance between him and the ranger station, ignoring how much daylight was being devoured. Now that uneasiness instantly returned, and he wished he hadn't looked at his watch.

Nine o'clock. Nearly five hours had flown by since he left Shawn and Mike.

He squeezed his fists against his forehead as if the pressure would squash down his bubbling feelings of despair. A small sob caught in his throat. The tiny noise was unbearably loud over the soft dripping of rain. Justin inhaled several deep breaths to master his emotions.

I don't have time for this. Shawn and Mike need me.

He bagged his map and stowed it safely in his pocket. Forcing himself to stand, he held out his compass once more to confirm his direction. He aimed to rebuild a hiking rhythm, but the forest floor was still uncertain – firm in some places, slippery in others.

He dug into his pocket again for more granola bar. A long time had passed since his last few bites after the moose. He talked himself out of eating the whole bar in case he didn't reach his destination soon. Carefully placing the final granola half back in his pocket, his fingers grazed his small LED flashlight. Soon he would need to rely on this tiny tool. The night was almost completely upon him, the darkness hurried along by the persistent rain clouds.

The forest denseness didn't help his vision either. Tree trunks created the borders of a dark maze for him to navigate and shut out what little light was left. He hooked his flashlight's keychain ring around his left little finger and nestled the compass in the palm of his right hand for frequent direction checks.

Finally, it happened. No matter how hard he squinted or shifted his body between the trees, there was no light left. In the absolute darkness, Justin felt more alone than he had for his entire journey. He tried to shake off the isolation.

What had changed? The only thing that's different now than a half hour ago is light. And the fact that everything in the forest that's awake right now can see except me. He couldn't help but nervously glance over his shoulder and flashback to every horror movie he'd ever watched. *Yep, in those movies the guy separated from his friends in the forest always 'gets it' first.*

He squared his shoulders and sped up slightly, determined not to let his imagination run wild. Just to be sure he'd escaped any forest surprises, he flicked his flashlight on the trail ahead and the trail behind. He sighed, both relieved and saddened. He *was* completely alone.

One thing had changed for the better. As he dodged dripping trees he realized that the rain had actually stopped. Not that it mattered much. He was already soaked through and chilled to the bone.

Reaching a tiny clearing, Justin checked his compass. The open space offered a glimpse of the sky, where a sprinkling of stars made an appearance between dispersing rain clouds. *Any kind of extra light would be really helpful.*

With the forest terrain and weather now cooperating, renewed energy and determination pushed Justin to cover more ground. Maybe his luck was changing. He even worked up a system of singing verses of his favorite songs in his head between flashlight and compass checks. Without relying as much on his sight he found himself attuned to how the ground felt under his squishy, moist boots, and how fresh and crisp the night air smelled.

His ears keenly evaluated each forest noise for signs of trouble over the low background noise of the Windermere in the distance. *This must be what it's like to be blind.*

More stars had gradually brightened the sky, but what extra light they lent to Justin's progress was short-lived. His last flashlight pass showed denser forest ahead. A flare of frustration burned in his chest. *Why can't things just go smoothly for more than two minutes?* Gritting his teeth, he willed himself forward.

Mom always said that no stretch of 'luck' lasted forever, so he should make his own luck. He really never understood exactly how he was supposed to do that, but on this journey it was becoming clearer.

The dense forest enveloped him, obscuring the tiny stars from his view. The heavy plant canopy trapped the moisture remaining from the rain, making his clothes feel wetter than they had five minutes ago. The ground surface was slicker under foot, and he had to slow his pace to feel some control. Brief flashlight sprays illuminated more erratic rock outcroppings that Justin zigzagged to avoid.

Despite the irregular path, Justin became confident in his methods of swerving the difficult footing and soon increased his speed. He relaxed his body into the rhythm, allowing his boots to roll easily with the loose rocks. His last light sweep illuminated a sparse grouping of rocks. Justin hopped between the rock spaces like hopscotch.

He had nearly cleared the obstacle course when his right foot landed on something soft and squishy.

SHRIEK!

Startled, Justin juggled his feet to avoid the small creature as it scuttled out from under him. His boots rolled uncontrollably over the loose rocks lining his path. His legs wobbled like jelly in response. He collapsed in half-time into a garbled pile on the uneven ground. Instinctively, he thrust his right hand forward to protect his weak knee from more battering. But the second he successfully defended his knee, Justin felt the compass fly from the palm of his hand.

"No!"

Forgetting his knee, he frantically pawed the ground with his protective hand. Thankfully the flashlight was still looped around his left baby finger to aid in his desperate search. Panic swelled every moment he scoured the forest floor for his precious tool with no results. Justin flashed the tiny light erratically in hopes the compass would reveal itself in the glow. But the debris blanketing the forest floor concealed the compass completely.

Justin slumped back on his heels. "It's gone," he said out loud, the volume of his voice sounding overblown.

The feelings of despair that he'd choked back many times on this journey threatened to take control again. Tears burned in his eyes, and his chest constricted with such frustration that he nearly screamed. But a quiet, reasonable voice inside his head slipped past the frustration and made him think twice.

That would be stupid. Every creature meaner than you in this forest would know exactly where you are.

Justin sucked in a huge breath and let it seep slowly between his clenched teeth. A pang in his troublesome knee reminded him that he was kneeling on the cold ground. Shifting into a more comfortable sitting position, weariness replaced frustration. He pulled out his final granola bar half.

About now I could eat both the roast beef and the macaroni and cheese.

Wishing for food and warmth, his thoughts traveled home. If Dad saw Justin sitting and crying, what would he say? *You're too weak, Justin. Jason would have been at the ranger station by now sipping hot chocolate. Justin, you're not trying hard enough.*

But that internal voice piped up again. *But you are trying your best.* Justin knew that's what Mom would say. *Your friends need your help. Don't give up – you're almost there. Like track and field in the relay race when your legs are on fire, but your teammates are depending on you to finish.* He knew the same was true now, only it wasn't just a race – it was their lives. He'd made it past the moose. He'd made it through the rocks and trees. And he could finish this journey without that compass.

He swallowed his final bite of granola. He hadn't realized how noisy his chewing or his thoughts were until he was done ruminating over both. The renewed silence tuned his ears to the forest night-sounds and the ever-present dull rush of the Windermere.

And that dull rush would keep him on track. A thrill surged inside him. The solution to his problem was right in front of his nose. Or rather, running right beside him.

I'll move closer to the river and follow its path the rest of the way to the ranger station. Hope began to edge out Justin's frustration. *It can't be more than a few more miles judging by my map.*

He shone his light on his carefully packaged map and marked his best estimate of his location. Tucking the map safely away, he heaved himself from the chilly ground. He pressed closer to the variable rocky edge of the river's course. The water's push against its stony borders filled his ears as a constant background noise. His progress was slower here than on the surer ground he'd left, but it wasn't as slippery as he thought.

Justin tried to regain some hiking rhythm. He continued his regular flashlight scans, and finally settled into a new determination. He would not let Mike and Shawn down. Not now that he was so close.

Maybe Dad was right. *He always thinks I can do better. And now I am pushing myself harder than I ever have. I'm not sure anyone would have guessed I'd be having this kind of extreme wilderness experience.* Dad had wanted Justin to come to camp to prepare for the family hunting trip. Mom thought Wapiti Junction would be fun for Justin because he loved outdoor sports. Justin was sure this situation exceeded the limits of Dad's idea of 'taking it to the edge.'

Justin remembered Mom telling him about when Dad was a kid. At the time he'd tried not to listen because he thought Mom was making excuses for Dad. She'd said something about Granddad getting injured and not being able to work for some time, so the family didn't have much money.

She'd explained that Dad went to high school, worked an after school job and refused to quit the hockey team. He'd counted on a hockey scholarship to support him at college because, although Granddad's small business did well enough, it still wouldn't cover every expense. Even after Granddad got better, Dad still didn't let go of that drive that pushed him through those harder times. He got the scholarship and kept a job even after he went to college. Mom said she thought he never wanted to have his opportunities threatened again.

Now in the loneliness of the pitch-black forest, navigating his way through his uncertain and unforgiving path, Justin thought differently about that conversation. *Maybe Mom was trying to explain why Dad was always so hard on me: always do as much as you can; never be unprepared.* She'd also tried to tell Justin that Dad just didn't want him to miss out on anything. *Interesting, but exactly whose opportunities am I missing out on – mine or his?*

Justin shook his head to clear the memory. He scanned his path in front and, just to be safe, he scanned the path behind. In either direction the shape of the forest was exactly the same in the dark. *I knew driving up here I never wanted to be lost in this bush.* At least he could depend on his ears to follow the river and not his eyes. 'Blind as a bat' was a phrase that now made much more sense.

CHAPTER 8

After half an hour of tracking the Windermere, Justin's modified way of navigating was proving successful. The terrain was less forgiving than deeper inside the treeline, but his progress was steady. Occasionally he felt like a mountain goat clambering over unstable rock piles. Those rough patches made his knee complain fiercely. Justin gritted his teeth and drove through the discomfort.

Without the insulation of the thicker brush and tree canopy farther from the Windermere's embankment, Justin was colder than when the rain assaulted him. His clothes and boots still hadn't completely dried, and numbness gripped his toes and fingers. Gritting his teeth with determination also kept them from chattering. The temperature drop pierced his aching knee like the freezing needles doctors used before stitching your sports injuries. He vaguely wondered if he was getting hypothermic.

The cold wasn't the only challenge. The weariness that plagued Justin since the loss of his compass weighted his boots to the earth and constantly threatened to stop him in his tracks altogether.

A fire and a rest would be nice. Justin figured he could scrounge enough semi-dry brush to raise a small fire to take the edge off the cold. But he quickly decided against stopping. Too much time had been wasted searching for the compass.

Well, Dad, during this trek I certainly have been 'applying myself'. Justin smiled wryly at how he'd finally achieved what Dad was always nagging him to do. And he wasn't even here to see it.

Just this past spring Dad had launched into one of his finest sermons, to inspire Justin to 'pull up his socks' before finals rolled around. Dad had intercepted a science quiz emblazoned with a huge red '79%' circled on top of the page. Justin had counted this test a success as he hadn't really studied, and he found the introductory geology section on rock composition pretty easy.

It made sense why tires gripped on some rocks easier while mountain biking, which is what Justin and his buddies were doing the weekend before the test. Dad, however, saw the grade as full proof that Justin had not given his best effort.

"If you had only studied a bit more you could have tipped that score into honors," Dad had said, looking disappointed.

This then lead to the whole 'Justin, you're smarter than this' and 'applying yourself will open more doors for you' lectures.

Justin knew he was smart. He understood the material in every subject at school without really having to read it more than once or twice. It just seemed that capturing all that extra detail took so much more effort with such little reward that it was not worth doing to score a couple of extra percent.

With Dad constantly after him, Justin occasionally felt guilty. But what would happen if Justin actually applied himself and still it wasn't enough? Wouldn't there always be room for improvement? What if 'better' still wasn't enough for Dad? Justin was certain he didn't want to disappoint Dad more than he already did. Because it wasn't just about science quizzes. What if Justin applied himself to the fullest and still didn't make it into law school or business school or whatever? The ultimate failing that would be.

No. No. Justin felt more like himself when he balanced his time spent at school with his time at sports. He had it down to an art, knowing just how much studying and practicing he could juggle to touch suitably on everything. No harm, no foul. No disappointment on anyone's part - other than Dad's. Mom didn't seem worried. She'd always back him by telling him to do his best and enjoy himself. Those kinds of expectations suited him best.

But now here he was, in a situation where applying himself meant the difference between life and… well, he didn't want to even think about the other option. Yet his body felt like he'd been in the butcher's meat freezer too long. The symptoms of hypothermia he'd learned about at camp kept flashing warning signals in his head.

He released his stubborn determination to trudge forward and decided to rest. He had to do something good for his body or soon it would do nothing for him. He had no food left, so a bit of warmth and rest was all there was to choose. He was no good to Mike and Shawn if something happened to him, so a bit or precious time devoted to his own well-being was necessary.

Near the rocky edge that crested the Windermere's steep embankment, enough wind gusts had stirred the deadfall to make them dry enough to tinder a fire. Justin reverently pulled out one match from the waterproof container and gently coaxed flames from the sparse branch pile. Carefully he tended the young fire, adding more branches and leaves only after he was sure it had caught. His actions reminded him of the fire he lit for Mike and Shawn before he left. His heart squeezed with anxiety about how they might be fairing. He couldn't fail them. Not now he was so close.

Lingering dampness in some pieces of deadfall made the fire smolder. The smoke smelled like the outdoor campfires lit for evening gatherings at Wapiti Junction.

Justin wished desperately for marshmallows and hot chocolate. One flaming marshmallow, crusty outside and gooey inside, would set him up for the next two miles. He sighed longingly, removed his boots and socks to dry and settled for simply warming his toes. Sometimes around the Wapiti fire it blazed so hot you couldn't stretch your legs too close, thinking the soles of your boots might melt. Everyone would complain and shove their log-seats back to a cooler spot. How good that heat would have felt right now!

The firelight cast a strange glow that performed a fleeting shadow show over the rocks that then vanished into the darkness of the trees. An owl hooted eerily, drawing Justin's attention back to the nighttime forest sounds that he'd tuned out with his concentration. The firelight exposed him again to the forest dwellers, but Justin didn't have the energy worry if anything would bother him. For most of his journey he'd been unnoticed and unseen, gradually melding with the forest itself.

Now if only I could be seen *as soon as possible by someone at the search and rescue station.*

He draped his leg over a rounded rock. His knee joint pulsated with swelling and overuse, but it was a great relief to rest it. He maneuvered a large rock behind his back and reclined as best he could. *Hardest armchair I've ever sat in.*

He stared into his built-up fire. It was quickly consuming its fuel, and soon Justin would need to be on his way. That was probably a good thing. Fire always had a way of relaxing and mesmerizing

Justin until he felt sleepy. And this was definitely no time for sleep, despite how much he wanted to give in and curl up by the warmth.

He roused himself to reach for his map. It was nice to be able to comfortably gauge his location and mark the time without needing to juggle his flashlight and pen. The time had unbelievably crept past the ten-thirty mark.

Gotta get moving. Time sure slides by when you can't afford to lose any.

He tested his socks. Still pretty moist but warmer than before. He winced as he stretched the damp hiking socks over his dry feet. There was almost nothing yuckier than putting your wet socks back on. The boots were not much drier, but Justin took what improvements he could get.

He smudged out the remnants of his little blaze, thanking it silently. He checked it twice to make sure it was extinguished before carrying on. Orienting the Windermere's bubbling rush on his left, he resumed his tracking habits by scanning his upcoming path with his LED. He heaved his leaden legs forward, disregarding the protests from his stiffened knee, and melted invisibly into the darkened landscape.

CHAPTER 9

*O*nly about twenty minutes had past since Justin's rest when the bone-weary fatigue descended again. The unpredictable rocky footing had not improved the farther he traveled. His knee now throbbed constantly as if the brief break had reminded it how mistreated it had been during this endless hike. His exhaustion and discomfort played heavily on his emotions. Each jarring step he took strangled more sobs of frustration in his throat. Temporarily stowed worry for Shawn and Mike leaked from the safe compartment he'd formed in his head down to his heart.

What if I'm too late? What if something else has happened to them, like a bear or the fire dying? Justin battled the overwhelming panic down by brushing the tears roughly from his eyes. But it was useless. The despair, frustration, fear and fatigue he'd controlled for the whole journey simultaneously attacked him, paralyzing him in his path.

Tears flooded like water through Windermere's rapids. Sobs racked his body in forceful waves. His weariness was so all-consuming his legs could no longer hold his weight. He slammed his palms against a larger boulder for support, and rode out the torrent of feelings. Then, as suddenly as it had overtaken him, the emotional storm dissipated. His recovery breaths and sniffling were unbearably loud as they echoed off his support boulder. To regain some control, he heaved an enormous sigh, and amazingly felt purged.

Why is this happening? He stared skyward wishing for some divine power to step into help him. That always seemed to work in science fiction movies – the hero usually is bestowed with some great power that frees him from an unbeatable situation.

And what about God? Didn't Granddad always say that God helped people who were trying to help themselves? Certainly Justin qualified for that. Not only was he trying to help himself, but Shawn and Mike as well. If Justin failed, his friends did not deserve to die out here. They'd been nothing but good friends to him. Surely God didn't let bad things happen to people who'd mostly done right in the world?

But no one had really ever been able to explain God's ways adequately to Justin. Granddad had tried when Grandma died. The whole family functioned best under her soothing influence, and yet she was gone. How Granddad had rationalized her early passing by saying, "God always takes the good ones sooner," wasn't enough. And younger Justin didn't ask any more questions, mostly because he didn't know what to ask. Now he didn't want Mike and Shawn to be two of those 'good ones' who went home to God just because his own quest to help them was going poorly.

Looking upward, he focused on a single bright star. He sent up a silent awkward prayer for his friends' safety and a good break for the rest of his mission. *Couldn't hurt to ask for help, or at least that's what Mom tells me.* Strangely enough, it also made him feel better.

But unfortunately he wasn't in that sci-fi movie. No special powers were forthcoming, and no alien force stood between him and his goal. No, it was Justin himself that was between Shawn and Mike's safety and perishing in the wilderness.

Justin collected his thoughts and the remnants of his physical strength and plunged onward. The search and rescue station had to be close. Grim determination replaced Justin's volatile emotions as he set a grueling pace toward his ultimate destination.

CHAPTER 10

The only two things Justin could hear were Windermere's rushing white noise and his own strained breathing. He honed in on these sounds to drown out the driving ache in his right knee.

His clothes were still partially damp from the rain, but they were getting worse from sweating. At least his body wasn't cold any more. Harder and harder he pushed, forcing himself over some of the most unpredictable terrain yet. His head and heart propelled him, overriding the physical fatigue he could not shake. If it were just up to his body, Justin would have collapsed about a kilometer back.

He arced his flashlight beam over his path more frequently so he could rapidly zigzag the worst of his trail. Tough luck if the LED burned out before he made it to the ranger station, but there was little sense in conserving power now.

He sensed the gradual slope increase the closer he moved to the station. He couldn't tell if he was breathing heavier just from driving himself or because of higher altitude. He knew the station was situated higher up the mountain. It needed to be to serve the ski slopes and heli-skiing as well as the foothills camps. No doubt the search and rescue team received more calls for snow-related accidents than hiking ones.

Justin grimaced. *If we had a ski accident at least I'd be traveling downhill right now.*

For the entire trail behind him, Justin had fought not to think of Shawn and Mike for fear of losing his nerve. Now he concentrated on picturing their faces, remembering the things they'd done together, to keep his relentless pace.

Justin focused on small goals, like making it in under five minutes to the next giant boulder, so he could celebrate success more often. Visualization was an exercise his basketball coach made the team practice on bus trips to away games. Coach guided the boys in imagining being on the other team's gym floor, tossing free throws and running offensive and defensive patterns. By the time the bus had arrived, they had often 'played' the game two or three times, excelling every time.

Justin didn't know exactly how the visualization improved their stats, but he did know he rarely felt nervous before a game.

Coach also told them to just play well and not to look at the clock, as that was his job. So Justin stopped looking at his watch, figuring the same applied now. Time didn't matter as much as just making it to the station in one piece to tell their story. Still he had a sense that it was probably approaching midnight, based on his last time check and his pace. All this dwelling on time and progress allowed stray thoughts wander into his head.

What if I can't wake anyone at the station when I get there? Or worse – what if they've been called out somewhere else? He caught himself at breaking his own rules and shook his head angrily. *No, don't be crazy. They probably always have at least one person left to man the station. And they are an emergency team used to waking up at weird hours to help someone.*

Justin beat down the negative thoughts farther by jogging through a clear stretch of ground. Rounding the trail that curved past the edge of a tightly spaced stand of lodgepole pine, a flicker of light grabbed his attention.

He stopped dead in his tracks, peering curiously between the thin, branchy trees. *Too low to the ground to be stars. Shiny animal eyes – wolf, maybe?* No, it was more stationary than a lurking forest creature.

Then hope nearly exploded from his chest. The light emanated from the ranger station!

From that point his eyes were fixed on the beautiful light piercing the wooded darkness. Justin shoved his flashlight into his leg pocket, keeping his hands free in grab trees and outcroppings to slingshot himself faster through the remaining trail. His legs were slaves to his desire to rapidly cover the ground between him and the light, no matter how many times he tripped or stumbled. Sometimes the light vanished behind a dense patch of trees, allowing panic to rise again. But a slight body shift once again revealed the elusive target in all its glory.

A few more meters. That's all that's left of this awful journey.

His breaths were ragged and his tattered shirt stuck to his sweaty back. Justin had forgotten his uncomfortably empty stomach and that he was ice-cold for most of trail before. He was consumed with the final leg of his trek as if it was all that ever existed.

Time lapsed elastically during the short minutes since he had sighted the light. At long last he could make out the pine-pole fence that skirted the station property. The entrance steps were *right there*. And the front door.

Just a bit more!

SMACK. With great momentum, his whole body thundered onto the ground, ending in a crumpled heap. The searing pain in his right knee that followed jolted him back to his presence in the forest. Hi mouth shaped an agonizing scream, but no sound came out. No water and hard breathing had robbed him of his voice. Clutching his twisted and trapped leg, he clenched his teeth and silently suffered the passing of the sudden injury shock from his abused joint. A few deep breaths and gentle massage offered a little more relief and the possibility of moving. He writhed around on the forest floor to free his right boot from the tree root it was wedged under.

Damn – not again! Couldn't have been the other leg. And I can't even yell for help.

But that ranger station door was within reach, injured knee or not. He dragged his ragged body up from the ground, grasping at limbs to relieve the load from his leg. Justin wished he had another one of Shawn's resourceful splints. The whole standing process was a huge ordeal as Justin could no longer bear nay weight on his knee. The surprise at only having one functional leg left him thrashing wildly to achieve balance. Branches snapped and rocks crunched under his boots as he noisily crashed his way to standing. He was upright just in time to see a sleek black shadow plowing toward him.

Grrrr! Bark, bark!

Oh God, all this and now *a wolf sees me!*

Justin nearly fainted from fright as the large canine bounded purposefully in his direction.

I can't die like this - not now!

Justin clung to his tree supports and clamped his eyes shut, waiting for the inevitable.

Sniff, sniff. Pant, pant.

No chewing or biting. Justin risked a peek out of one partially opened eye. The intelligent, regal face of a German shepherd regarded him curiously, head tilted to one side.

"Help me," he managed to croak before crashing weakly to the ground.

The dog seemed to understand. He instantly spun around, barking constantly back to the station door. Justin watched breathlessly as the dog pawed and clawed the outer screen door until it opened.

"What's wrong, boy? You see something?" A man leaned out the door and peered around.

Another human!

Justin's anticipation swelled while the dog coaxed the man from the station, barking and bouncing back and forth along Justin's direction.

"All right. Let me get my boots and flashlight."

Mirroring Justin's despair, the dog whined worriedly as the man slipped his boots on and powered up his lantern flashlight.

The shepherd bounded back toward Justin, forcing the man to run to keep up.

"This better not be a squirrel, Jethro," he said, lifting his lantern for a better look. "My coffee's getting cold…"

The man stopped dead in his tracks as the light washed over Justin's crumpled form.

"Help. My friends. The river," was all Justin could choke out in his raspy-whisper voice, now strangled with sobs.

"My God!" the man rushed forward for a better look. "We've got you!" He raised his lantern to quickly scan the surrounding bush. Satisfied there was no one else in the immediate area, the man turned his attention back to Justin.

"Don't move. I'll be right back with more help for you," he said, the surprise of finding a boy instead of a squirrel wearing off his face. "Then we'll hear about your friends. Jethro, guard the boy."

Justin felt the dog curl protectively around him, and he began to feel that things might be changing for the better. Tears and sweat burned his eyes as he tried to focus on the man racing back to the station, hollering for several other people and a stretcher. Justin leaned gratefully into Jethro's warm fur and rested. Then he couldn't help himself. He flung his arms around the dog's thick neck, hugging him tightly. Jethro didn't mind the attention and happily licked Justin's streaky face in return.

The following brief minutes were a blur of activity. Four men poured from the ranger station, carrying a stretcher, blankets and flashlights. They swarmed over Justin like ants at a picnic. The rangers talked constantly to him, explaining what they were doing, but he could muster little in response. He relied on nodding his head in acknowledgement, but managed to gesture that his knee was injured. He cooperated in every way possible, hoping fervently that they'd soon finish with him so he could tell them about Shawn and Mike.

"Relax, Jethro, we'll take him now," the first man said, rewarding the dog with a small treat from his pocket.

The team neatly rolled Justin onto the blanket-lined stretcher, sandwiching him under more blankets. Justin figured barely five minutes had passed since his rescuers had barreled out the station door until he was hustled back over the threshold. True indoor heat enveloped him like sauna steam.

The four men set the stretcher down beside a cozy couch, each grasping a corner of the bottom blanket. At the count of three they raised Justin onto the couch in one smooth movement.

Justin sank gratefully into the soft blankets and cushions, and allowed the men to efficiently minister to him. One propped his back with pillows and another did the same for his injured leg. The third brought a bag filled with ice cubes that he draped gently over Justin's knee. A mug of hot tea was secured in his hand. Jethro curled up on a frayed polar fleece throw beside the couch as if to monitor Justin's condition for the rangers.

The ranger who found Justin drew up an armchair and surveyed him. "I'm Rick, and that's Allen, Pete and Brian. We're the search and rescue technicians here at Sierra Station," he said quietly, as if he worried about spooking Justin. "Tell me about you and your friends…"

"My friends are in trouble down the river!" Justin finally blurted out hoarsely. "One is badly injured!"

Justin had barely finished his sentence before the other search and rescue technicians sprung into action, furiously organizing necessary clothing and equipment in the entrance way. Rick turned gravely back to Justin.

"First, is anything other than your knee seriously injured?" he asked. "Then we need to know everything you can tell us about your friends."

Justin quickly gulped more tea, its warmth and wetness coating his parched throat. When he spoke again, thankfully more strength had returned to his voice.

"No, I'm OK," he said, the words tumbling out rapidly. "My knee is the worst. Mostly I'm cold, tired and hungry. But my friends really need help!"

No longer caring about his raw throat, Justin's tale flooded from him, beginning with the canoe capsize and ending with meeting Jethro in the bush.

Rick regarded Justin with awe for a few seconds while the other rangers exchanged amazed glances over their rescue preparations.

Justin looked expectantly to each ranger, waiting for his story to sink in. "And I have my own map so I can show you where they are!" He fished into his pocket and produced the well-preserved map.

The rangers hauled over the long coffee table and quickly gathered around. Justin shifted his position on the couch so he could easily describe his map.

Seeing his completed field map for the first time in full light, he was surprised at how clear each of his additions was. Maybe his diligent updates would actually lead the rangers directly to Mike and Shawn. He started his explanation from the estimated crash site, describing what forest and terrain details he remembered along the entire course. Rick fetched one of the station's standard area maps and unrolled it on the coffee table.

"Let's see if we can match your map to ours," he said, tracing his finger along the Windermere's path. "Then we can better pinpoint your friends' location."

He rotated and shifted Justin's map along the area map, while everyone tossed out comments about possible location matches. Justin waited breathlessly, offering more detail where he could, as the rescue team expertly narrowed down a search grid. The closer they got to the best estimate of Mike and Shawn's location, the more Justin was able to relax.

Jethro's sniffing wet nose on his elbow drew his attention to a still-steaming bowl of oatmeal and brown sugar on the coffee table corner. *When did that get there?* He gave into his hunger and began devouring the bowl's contents. It was the best oatmeal he had ever tasted. Jethro looked disappointed.

"Sorry, boy, but I'm starving," he whispered to the dog, offering an ear scratch in exchange. A hoot of happiness from one of the rangers snapped him back to the discussion.

"That's got to be it," Brian said, tapping his finger on a small section of the area map. "Or at least it's the best place to start looking."

Rick looked pleased as he rolled up the area map. "Right. Let's get going."

The rescue team grabbed their assembled gear and scrambled to leave so quickly that Justin reeled in their wake. *They're gonna go without me!*

"I want to go with you," Justin begged. "I worked all this time to find help for my friends. I can't just sit here and do nothing but wait for you to find them." He looked pleadingly at each ranger, each of whom was shaking his head. "But they're *my* friends, and it was my responsibility to bring help. Please let me help you look."

Rick still looked doubtful. "What about your knee?"

"It's fine. I promise to keep the ice on it."

Pete and Brian shrugged, and Rick sighed in resignation. "All right. We could always use an extra set of eyes up there."

Justin's heart leapt. He grinned his thanks and prepared to get off the couch. Then he began to wonder about what Rick said. *Up where?*

Rick tossed a hooded sweatshirt to Justin and disappeared into a back room. He returned carrying fresh wool socks and a worn pair of hiking boots. "These should do for now."

He helped Justin change his right sock and shoe, and then offered his arm for support. He hobbled out the door with Rick as his crutch. Concentrating on the ground, he carefully watched where he placed his feet.

The path was wide, well-worn and well-lit, so there wasn't much to stumble on. Justin knew the other rangers passed him several times, carrying armloads of equipment. The path spread into an open flat piece of ground circled with floodlights. Justin finally raised his head to see Brian and Pete securing the last equipment packs into a large search and rescue helicopter.

"A helicopter!" Justin exclaimed, watching Allen move into the pilot's seat and hook on his headgear.

Rick laughed at Justin's surprise. "You didn't think we were going downstream in a speed boat, did you?"

CHAPTER 11

The helicopter ride was practically the most thrilling thing Justin had ever done. If their mission hadn't been so serious, he'd have truly enjoyed himself. As it was he was happier just to be getting closer to helping Mike and Shawn.

With the helicopter's searchlight flooding the ground below, he had a bird's eye view of his unforgiving trail. From up in the sky it was spectacular; from down on the ground it was torturous. The Windermere River itself was something to behold, even in the dark. Shawn would love this – just like a photo spread from *National Geographic*. Justin stomach turned at the thought of Shawn. His anxiety about finding his friends grew, but he was more certain now it would happen than he had been through his entire journey.

He was comfortably warm in his borrowed sweatshirt and from the cupful of thermos hot chocolate he received when they were airborne. During the time before they entered the search area, Rick firmly wrapped Justin's knee with a tensor bandage from one of the rescue kits. Pete discovered a package of trail mix in his vest pocket and happily presented it to Justin.

They hadn't flown long when Allen slowed the helicopter's speed to begin the sweep search. Justin was stunned by how little time it took to fly within searching range and how long it took him to cover the same distance on foot. He hoped that time span didn't make or break Shawn and Mike's chances of survival.

Everyone manned a window. Rick slid open the side door and positioned himself securely at the opening for a better view. With sunrise a couple of hours away, the ground still was dark and shadowy, even with the bright searchlight.

Justin absorbed everything he saw. Mentally, he compared how their makeshift campsite looked on land to how it would look from the sky. His anxiety deepened as the searching time stretched on without success. He eavesdropped nervously each time Rick and Allen conferred over the headsets. The more of the search pattern they completed, the sicker Justin became. But he had begged to come, and this was better that waiting uselessly back at the station.

"I've got them!" Rick yelled at last. "Small campfire, two people, 10 o'clock."

Justin's eyes zoned in on that spot, praying for immediate proof of life. He was rewarded with the sight of Shawn frantically waving his arms. Relief washed over him. At least Shawn was OK. And he knew the rangers would do their best for Mike.

Once the helicopter established hovering position, Justin did his best to stay out of the way and let the team do its job. Rick secured his gear and rapidly rappelled from the helicopter. Pete and Brian lowered a metal stretcher and equipment case into Rick's outstretched hands. Finally, Brian lowered himself to the ground and headed straight for Mike.

Justin watched Rick wrap a blanket around Shawn's shoulders. As they talked, Rick motioned toward the helicopter, and Shawn waved again. *Shawn must have asked about me.* Then he knew Shawn must be giving Rick details about Mike's condition, because Rick nodded and ran over to help Brian with the stretcher.

Justin nearly jumped out of his skin when Pete suddenly tapped his shoulder. "Rick called up to Allen. He says your friend is pretty bad off, but still alive." Justin smiled as Pete clapped him supportively on the back.

In no time Mike's stretcher was winched into the helicopter. Pete maneuvered it carefully through the door and secured it to the floor. He hooked up more basic life support measures on Mike. Mike looked pale and sweaty, and his breathing was shallow – but definitely alive. Justin was more satisfied now that he had seen for himself. He glanced worriedly at Pete, who offered a reassuring smile.

Next Shawn was strapped into a harness and winched into the helicopter. Justin waited as he unhooked himself, as the harness was not much different from a climbing one. Justin and Shawn hugged each other tightly.

"Thanks, man," Shawn said, wiping a stray tear. "I knew you wouldn't let us down."

Soon Rick and Brian were back on board, and everyone prepared to fly. Justin pulled off his borrowed sweatshirt and gave it to Shawn, and passed him a warm cup of thermos cocoa. Shawn sipped it slowly, savoring every mouthful. Rick gave Shawn a thumbs-up after a quick in-flight check up, and handed him a package of trail mix. Shawn gratefully dug into it immediately.

"We'll be landing at the hospital just down the mountain from Wapiti Junction," Rick yelled over the helicopter's drone. "We'll get word to your folks from there."

For the rest of the flight Justin and Shawn were content to sit side by side in silence. Relief and weariness soon consumed them, and they slept.

Justin jerked awake as the helicopter touched down. The next minutes were filled with a flurry of activity as doctors and nurses transferred them from the helicopter to the hospital. Justin barely had the chance to thank Rick and the other rangers before he was rushed away in a wheelchair.

They were thoroughly examined, and placed in beds to rest and recover. Justin and Shawn were both hooked up with intravenous saline drips to treat their exhaustion and dehydration. By this time they had told their stories several times. Each time more hospital staff stopped to listen in on the amazing tale. When the onslaught of technicians finished taking blood samples and readings, and the visits from other well-wishers died down, they had the chance to ask their main nurse, Marlene, about Mike.

"You boys saved his life," she said earnestly. "Without Shawn's first aide and Justin's gutsy trek to the SAR station, Mike wouldn't be with us now." She adjusted a lever on Shawn's fluid drip. "Right now he's in surgery for his leg, and we'll know more in a little while."

"We'd like to see him as soon as we can," Justin said.

Marlene smiled. "I'm sure that can be arranged, especially for you two. Mike's brother is coming in two days, and he says he can't thank you both enough for what you've done. Your parents will be here by tomorrow."

Shawn seemed pleased, but Justin was sure the last thing Dad wanted was to come up here prematurely and find the situation less than perfect. However, seeing Mom would make it all worthwhile, so he decided to worry about Dad's reaction when the time came. He sat back and enjoyed being safe and comfortable.

He and Shawn had a small television in one corner of their room, on which they promptly found the sports channel. They were moaning over a missed golf shot when breakfast arrived.

A kitchen staff member cheerily placed trays of toast, oatmeal, juice and tea on their bedside tables and added two bowls of fruit salad.

"Breakfast time already? Seems like just a couple of hours ago I was dining on trail mix," Shawn joked. Justin shook his head at him. He'd missed Shawn's unshakable sense of humor.

They were devouring their final bites when a new nurse poked her head into their room.

"Hello, boys. So you're the two newest heroes around here.

I'm Brenda, and I'll be taking care of you for the next shift. Nurse Marlene, said you should be kept up to date on your friend's condition," she said, checking their monitors and unhooking their intravenous drips. "The surgeon's team says he's out of surgery and is stable. So far it looks like they were able to make an excellent repair on his leg. He should be awake later this morning, and then we'll see about a quick visit."

"Thanks for telling us," Shawn said, as she briefly checked the dressings on the minor cuts and abrasions he had.

She moved on to Justin's knee. "My pleasure. Your last sets of lab tests came back good, so your doctor freed you from your IV's," she said, frowning as she checked the knee for bruising and swelling. "But you both look like you could use more toast. Should I see what the kitchen has leftover?"

Justin winced as Brenda rewrapped his bandage. "Yes, please. Anything you can find would be great. We haven't had our usual amount of food in the last day or so," Justin said.

Good to her word, Brenda reappeared a few minutes later with more toast and jam and bowls of dry cereal with milk. "After you eat, you boys should get some rest. I promise to get you when you can visit your friend."

They followed Brenda's advice to the letter, enjoying their second breakfast as heartily as the first, and easily falling into a lengthy deep sleep.

The faint crinkling of plastic woke Justin a few hours later. Through heavy eyelids he saw a nurse's aide place a huge fruit basket on the side table. He sat up, rubbing the sleep from his eyes. "Thanks," he said quietly.

"Oh, sorry," she whispered apologetically. "It's from your instructors at Wapiti Junction. Camp Nurse Gail brought it when she came to visit, but you were asleep. She decided to leave the basket and come back later."

"That would be great. I'm sure she wants to see that I didn't ruin my knee totally." He mustered a sleepy smile as the aide quietly excused herself.

Justin then tried unsuccessfully to wake Shawn by staring at him. *That guy could sleep through a tornado.*

Justin was glad to be awake when Brenda arrived carrying a jug of water and a small cup of tablets for Justin.

"Good, you're awake," she said, making sure he downed his medication. "Mike is awake and asking to see you both. His doctor says he could manage a short visit."

The perfect excuse to drag Shawn back from dreamland.

Justin heaved one of his pillows at Shawn's head.

"What the – hey!" Shawn squawked, sitting bolt upright.

"Get up, man, we can go see Mike," Justin said, laughing at Shawn's disorientation.

Brenda rolled in the wheelchair she'd brought for Justin, and soon they were headed to Mike's recovery room. Justin prepared himself on the short ride in case Mike was really in bad shape.

As Brenda parked him alongside Mike's bed, he was relieved to see Mike looking well. His leg was elevated slightly and encased in a huge cast. A thick white bandage covered the injury on his head and many other bruises were visible on his arms and shoulders. A thin oxygen tube ran into his nose and he was hooked to a couple of other monitors and drips that beeped regularly.

Brenda helped Shawn pull up another chair. "I'll be back in a few minutes," she said quietly closing the door behind her.

"Mike," Justin said softly.

Mike's eyes fluttered open and a smile crossed his face. "Hey, you guys. How are you doing?" His voice sounded tired and hoarse, but well enough, considering what he had been through.

"We're good," Shawn answered. "Well, actually I feel great, but Justin's knee is wrecked again."

"The sacrifices I make for my friends." Justin waved off his injury airily, but suddenly became serious. "And I'd do it all over again if I needed to. Is your leg going to be OK?"

"It will take weeks of sitting still and then more weeks of physiotherapy, but the surgeon says I should get full use back," he said. "Thanks to both of you. More than one staff member has told me everything you guys did for me."

Shawn shrugged. "It was the way you trained us, Mike." "You showed us how to be prepared and resourceful."

"So, do you think we passed our final challenge?" Justin asked jokingly.

Mike started laughing and grimaced in pain. "Ow, laughing makes my leg hurt."

Soon they were each telling their version of the tale. When Brenda poked her head into the room to escort the boys back, they were enjoying themselves so much that she offered to return in another fifteen minutes.

CHAPTER 12

The next morning Justin and Shawn's camping gear arrived from Wapiti Junction, as they were heading straight home from the hospital when their parents arrived. By yesterday evening, almost all of their instructors, a few co-campers and Nurse Gail had made visits.

Justin was absolutely shocked when Todd and Steven showed up unexpectedly. They asked about Mike and had wanted to hear the tale first hand. When they were about to leave, Steven commented that he was glad it wasn't him and Todd out there, because they probably wouldn't have made it. He laughed it off by saying they were better off facing the younger campers than facing the elements.

Then Justin and Shawn made one more visit to Mike before they were banished to bed by the returning nurse, Marlene. The three friends talked about sports and school and what they'd do when they got home, and made plans to keep in touch. If Mike was well enough to instruct again at Wapiti Junction next summer, he'd see about having Shawn and Justin hired as junior instructors. Their growing legend at camp would go a long way in impressing upon younger campers to pay careful attention.

When visiting hours were over, Marlene made sure Shawn and Justin were entrenched in their own room. They watched more sports channel and talked until they dropped off to sleep well after midnight. So when their camping gear noisily arrived the same time the breakfast trays were clanking against the metal trolley, Justin knew they should have gone to sleep earlier.

Shawn's mom arrived shortly after the boys finished dressing and inhaling their double-sized breakfasts. Her face was a mask of worry until she saw Shawn with her own eyes. She was only a little taller than her son, but she scooped him into an enormous hug, which Shawn returned enthusiastically. Then she gripped his shoulder and held him at arms' length and examined him suspiciously.

"Are you sure you're all right?" she asked, leveling a stern gaze – the kind you couldn't lie to – directly at Shawn.

"I've got lots of bruises and scratches, and I'm still hungry, but mostly I'm good. Justin and Mike took the worst of it," he answered truthfully, glancing at Justin.

She turned her genuine smile to Justin and promptly scooped him into one of those enormous hugs. "Justin. Thank you so much for everything you did. How is your knee?" she asked, looking him over the same way she did her own son.

"I'm OK, Ms. Miller. But I don't think there'll be much hockey for me this season." He was struck by how much Shawn looked like her – the same wavy, sandy blond hair and easy smile.

"Well, since you'll have some free time, you can spend some days with us on school breaks," she said, helping Justin sit on his bed to rest his knee. "We don't live too far away, do we, Shawn?"

Shawn grinned. "Thanks, Mom."

She gathered up some of Shawn's bags. "I'll take these out to the car. I'm sorry we have to leave you in such a rush, Justin, but Shawn's grandma is desperate to see for herself that he's OK. I'll give your parents a call when everything settles down. Maybe you can even come for Labor Day weekend before school starts."

"Thanks, Ms. Miller. I'd like that," Justin said.

She gave him that easy smile again. "Look after that knee," she said, and slipped out the door.

"I guess I'd better go," Shawn said reluctantly.

"Yeah. Better not keep your mom waiting," Justin replied, feeling suddenly empty and alone. Mastering his feelings, he stood and offered Shawn his hand.

Shawn clasped it firmly. "It's been an adventure, man. See you for Labor Day? I'll wheel you over to the skateboard park in a wagon, if I have to."

"Maybe I'll bring a quad. That way I can drive myself and still look cool."

Shawn clapped Justin's shoulder and smiled. "Take care." He grabbed his remaining bags and was gone.

Justin boosted himself back onto his bed and flipped on the television. Watching golf wasn't nearly as fun without Shawn helping him critique the shots. Thankfully Nurse Brenda arrived before Justin became ultimately bored with the game. She presented him with his regular dose of medication for knee pain and swelling, and a snack of two muffins and chocolate milk.

"Your parents should be here shortly," she said fluffing his pillows and readjusting his knee position.

"It's OK. I've got food and TV. What else could I need?"

Brenda patted his arm and handed him the remote control.

Halfway through the first tennis match he found, his mom rushed into the room. She looked worried, tearful and relieved all at the same time. She hurried to the bedside and hugged him tightly.

"Oh, Justin, thank God you're all right," she said, eying his many bandaged cuts and wincing over his thickly wrapped knee. "How are your friends?"

"Shawn is good. His mom came for him about an hour ago. And Mike is doing better. They fixed his leg and in time it will be as good as new," he answered. He was glad that Mom was finally there. "Where's Dad?" *Might as well get the inevitable over and done with.*

"We talked to your doctor to see what treatment and follow-up were needed for your knee, and then he wanted to stop and see Mike," she said, gently brushing his hair from his eyes. Then she paused. "He was really worried about you."

Justin shrugged. "Doesn't matter now. I'm fine."

As if on cue, Dad walked cautiously into the room. Justin was surprised to see Dad looking a bit haggard. *Maybe he really was worried about me.*

Mom stood up to change places with Dad. His eyebrows knit together as he looked over Justin's knee. He sat awkwardly on the bed's edge. "How are you, Jus? That knee looks painful."

"I'm fine, Dad. As long as I stay off the leg as much as possible and take my meds," Justin answered. He avoided looking at Dad, and waited for the upcoming lecture. However, he could not have predicted what happened instead.

Dad suddenly leaned in and clutched Justin in a fierce hug. Justin recovered his wits in time to properly hug him back. Over Dad's shoulder he looked questioningly at Mom, who simply smiled tearfully. At length, Dad released him.

"Mike told me how well you boys handled yourselves," Dad said. "Rick from the search and rescue station even called me to say what an amazing kid you are." He paused, looking squarely at Justin. "You did good, son."

"Thanks. 'Extreme outdoor experience' means something different to me now than it did before I came to camp."

"The last two weeks didn't actually play out the way any of us expected, did they?" Dad smiled.

Justin paused, gathering up some courage. "Dad, after all this, I really don't think the family hunting trip is for me."

Dad nodded slowly. "Given what you've been through, I think we can consider your wilderness experience complete – probably more complete than Granddad's or Jason's or mine put together."

Justin breathed a sigh of relief. "Can we go home now?"

"The sooner, the better," answered Mom, quickly gathering some of Justin's gear.

After a rounding the ward to thank the hospital staff, Dad pushed Justin's wheelchair out to the parking lot. He carefully loaded Justin into the back seat of the Jeep and propped his knee comfortably. Mom and Dad chatted happily as they jostled down the remainder of the mountain trail. Out the rear windshield Justin stared at the passing treeline, still solidly concealing the forest's mysteries. *Well, maybe not quite as many mysteries now.* As for the rest, Justin really didn't need to know.

CPSIA information can be obtained
at www.ICGtesting.com
Printed in the USA
LVHW091342250219
608668LV00001B/190/P